I0720397

His Majesty's Hounds – Book 5

Sweet and Clean Regency Romance

Enchanting the Duke

Arietta Richmond

Dreamstone Publishing © 2017

www.dreamstonepublishing.com

ISBN-13: 978-1-925499-56-8

Books by Arietta Richmond

His Majesty's Hounds

Claiming the Heart of a Duke

Intriguing the Viscount

Giving a Heart of Lace (a prequel to Winning the Merchant Earl)

Being Lady Harriet's Hero

Enchanting the Duke (coming soon)

Redeeming the Marquess (coming soon)

Healing Lord Barton (coming soon)

Winning the Merchant Earl (coming soon)

Loving the Bitter Baron (coming soon)

Rescuing the Countess (coming soon)

Attracting the Spymaster (coming soon)

The Derbyshire Set

A Gift of Love (Prequel short story)

A Devil's Bargain (Prequel short story - coming soon)

The Earl's Unexpected Bride

The Captain's Compromised Heiress

The Viscount's Unsuitable Affair

The Count's Impetuous Seduction

The Rake's Unlikely Redemption

The Marquess' Scandalous Mistress

A Remembered Face (Bonus short story – coming soon)

The Marchioness' Second Chance (coming soon)

A Viscount's Reluctant Passion (coming soon)

Lady Theodora's Christmas Wish

The Duke's Improper Love (coming soon)

Other Books

The Scottish Governess (coming soon)

The Earl's Reluctant Fiancée (coming soon)

The Crew of the Seadragon's Soul Series, (coming soon - a set of 10 linked novels)

Dedication

For everyone who had the grace to be patient while this book, and every other book that I have written, was coming into existence, who provided cups of tea, and food, when the writing would not let me go, and endured countless times being asked for opinions.

For the readers who inspire me to continue writing, by buying my books! Especially for those of you who have taken the time to email me, or to leave reviews, and tell me what you love about these books, and what you'd like to see more of – thank you – I'm listening, I promise to write more about your favourite characters.

For my growing team of beta readers and advance reviewers – it's thanks to you that others can enjoy these books in the best presentation possible!

And for all the writers of Regency Historical Romance, whose books I read, who inspired me to write in this fascinating period.

ARIETTA RICHMOND

Chapter One

The County of Berkshire, England – late March 1815

The crisp Spring air carried the last frosts of winter across the bleak countryside and nipped the exposed cheeks of the burly coach driver who steered the stately coach carefully through the wide wrought iron gates and into the grounds of Casterfield Grange. Frost-covered poplars lined the gravelled driveway and groundsmen in warm, long, woollen coats touched their hats in respect as the coach rolled by, wheels clattering on the small pebbles and steam swirling from the backs of the tired horses.

"Finally," whispered Lady Cordelia Branley, the elder daughter of the Baron whose family had held the noble title of Tillingford for nearly eight hundred years. She pushed her hands deeper into the fox-fur muff that kept her hands protected from the cold and smiled.

"Home at last and we have arrived whilst it is still daylight."

Her companion (once her governess) tried to smile, but looked tired from the journey.

Miss Millpost was a strict and severe spinster of some fifty summers, a woman whose main responsibility was to chaperone the pretty, dark haired seventeen-year old girl, teach her how to run a household as only a good and obedient wife should, and keep her out of mischief. The companion shifted her bony frame on the hard, leather-bound coach seat.

"How may we even know if the sun still exists beyond those dark clouds and the bitter cold? If I don't have warm tea to revive me, child, I fear I shall expire from the ague!"

Lady Cordelia tried not to laugh, for she knew that Miss Millpost would sooner revive her spirits with a glass or two of her father's excellent Madeira.

She sighed. It felt good to be home once more, and she was more than excited to see her loving father again and her beautiful younger sister, Georgiana.

Ever since their dear mama had died, in a cholera epidemic when Georgiana was only five, and Cordelia seven, Cordelia had tried to assume the role of mother, and she naturally felt deeply protective of her sister.

The younger girl often behaved more like a boy and had seemed to prefer playing in the garden and getting herself covered in mud and leaves rather than learning to embroider and excel at the feminine arts. But their father loved them both dearly and indulged them in whatever ways might make them happy.

Despite the constant shadow of their mother's tragic death, it was still a happy household and a wonderful place to grow up.

Georgiana's insatiable curiosity had even prompted her father to consider appointing a tutor for his younger daughter and he was weighing the issue in his comfortable library with a pipe of fine Virginia tobacco and glass of good cognac when he heard the carriage wheels and the horses' hooves approaching the house.

Clouds of hot breath surrounded the horses as they pulled the carriage across the frosted ground and finally slowed to a welcome halt outside the grand entrance portico of Baron Tillingford's elegant home. Servants hurried to open the carriage door and unfold the steps so that the passengers could alight. They were smiling as Cordelia stepped down, obviously pleased to see her Ladyship safely returned from her journey. They fussed around her, almost ignoring the companion as she struggled to step down without lifting the hem of her heavy skirt and revealing her bony ankles. It was important to observe the correct proprieties at all times, she felt. Especially in front of the servants.

"Papa!" Cordelia cried as she caught sight of her father at the top of the steps. She raced up the broad stone stairs and hugged the Baron, who could barely contain his tears of joy as he held his lovely daughter in his arms and gave thanks for her safe return.

"You look so much like your beloved mama, my dear. How can I look upon you and not see the radiance of her grace and beauty? It warms my heart and cheers my soul!"

The companion coughed loudly behind Cordelia's back to announce her presence.

"Miss Millpost. Well met and welcome back. You must join me in the library for a glass of light refreshment and tell me how went your visit to London."

Cordelia had not long celebrated her seventeenth birthday and the Baron had finally bowed to pressure from his precious elder daughter and allowed her to visit relatives in London. The Baron's cousin was an influential woman and a well-known and popular guest in the salons and elegant drawing rooms of London's high society. Sadly, her husband had died a little more than a year ago, of an apoplexy, and whilst she was well off, she was, it had seemed to the Baron, rather lonely. Cordelia's visit was a boon for both of them. She had provided the perfect opportunity to introduce Cordelia to the nobility of the nation's capital.

At seventeen, the Baron was also aware that his daughter would soon be eligible for marriage and that it would do no harm for her pretty face and lovely smile to be seen in the discerning circles of the gentry. The hard fact was that the endless wars with Napoleon had taken far too many young men away from England's shores to offer their service in His Majesty's Army and Navy. And too few of them ever came back.

The result was that there simply were not so many young, eligible noblemen around who might come to Baron Tillingford and seek Cordelia's hand in marriage. Introducing the young woman into London society might possibly draw the attention of a noble young suitor, and then the ageing Baron could rest easier in the knowledge that at least one of his daughters had made a good match. It was all he wanted for his girls. To see them happily married and presiding over a great and noble household.

For, as he sadly had no son to follow him, the Barony, and its entailed estates, would pass to someone else, probably some extremely distant relative, or someone chosen by the King, as he had, to his knowledge, no male relatives to succeed him.

That made it all the more important that his girls be well placed with suitable husbands. He could leave them Casterfield Grange, for it was not entailed, nor were a few other properties he held, including the house in Bath where his great aunt Petrina had lived out her life as a spinster, so their beloved home would still be theirs when he was no longer here to care for them. Still, he wished to see them happy, and married to men of suitable wealth and breeding, as soon as possible.

It wasn't too much to ask for, but the Baron was aware of his age and his growing infirmity. Time, he felt, was not on his side.

Chapter Two

London had been a revelation for the young Lady Cordelia Branley. She had danced until her feet hurt, charmed and excited by being so much in demand, and flushed with the attention of so many gentlemen. She had found many of those attentive gentlemen rather too old for her liking, and many were not so handsome of figure, no matter how elegantly dressed. Still their attention was flattering, and it was obvious that her beauty stood out amongst the girls present, with her striking dark hair and fresh skin. Many of the younger men seemed to avoid the dancing, perhaps because their families were pushing them to marry? Their absence initially disappointed her, but Cordelia soon discovered where they were hiding themselves during most of the Balls.

She'd been thrilled to see the well-dressed young bucks in their expensively-tailored attire, seated around card tables and wagering loudly on the outcome of every hand. Whilst the card rooms at Balls were more commonly frequented by men, and a few of the older ladies, only, Cordelia had begged her hostess for a chance to see what went on.

The games had been exciting to watch and, one evening, when one of the young nobles spied Cordelia and nodded his head at her with a courteous smile, it was all that she could do to contain herself. She blushed and the young man laughed, his carefully-oiled mass of dark curls set off with a black silk ribbon tied in a bow at the back.

He looked back at the table and roared with delight as he turned the final card and gathered up his winnings. His companions groaned as they threw their cards on the table and Cordelia turned to her hostess and asked who the young man might be.

"That is Lord Edward Fitzhugh, second son of the Earl of Bolton, my dear, a fine young man who should be alongside his father in the King's uniform, fighting the French in Spain. But he prefers to spend his days slug-a-bed and his nights gambling at the card tables and carousing."

Her hostess' voice was severe, quite disapproving, but she refused to say more on the matter. With her heart beating and her pretty eyes widening, Cordelia was utterly convinced that he was by far the most handsome young man she had seen.

Ever.

~~~~~

To one side of the room, an older gentleman, handsome, elegant and exquisitely presented, in attire that was in no way ostentatious, yet spoke, in its every line, of the best tailoring that money could buy, leant against the wall watching the room.
~~~~~

∿∿∿∿∿

Philip Canterwood, Duke of Rotherhithe, enjoyed a hand of cards, but never gambled with any serious intent. He had just finished a game with some acquaintances, and now simply stood, quietly, watching. The behaviour of men when they gambled intrigued him.

The room was full of extravagantly dressed young fops, eager to display their wealth an unconcern for its loss, hoping, at every turn, to impress the young ladies who watched wide eyed. The fops might not yet wish to be captured into marriage, but they were hungry for a woman's admiration.

His gaze travelled around the room, alighting on a face he did not know. Beside Lady Mathilde Egremont stood a girl he had never seen before. She was young, and innocent inexperience showed in everything about her. But she was outstandingly beautiful, with rich dark hair, and glowing pale skin. Her lips, currently open in a small gasp, as one of the fops looked her way, were a delightful dark pink that fair begged to be kissed, if one were a man prone to kissing innocents.

Not usually one to be interested in the young girls, barely past childhood, that the mothers of the ton paraded in hopes of snaring a husband, he yet found himself watching this girl closely. Something about her drew him, as if, in some way, she might be different from the others.

He shook his head at his whimsy, and turned back to conversation with some friends, with a last faint wondering at who she might be.

∿∿∿∿∿

During the following days, Cordelia conspired with her hostess to attend as many social functions as possible, overtly to meet as many noble ladies and gentlemen as she could but secretly with the hope that she might catch sight, once more, of the dashing Lord Edward Fitzhugh. Her hopes were not in vain.

Many of the great salons offered cards and the sport of wagering on the outcome, a pursuit that might have been reserved for the candlelit interiors of the gentlemen's clubs, but was widely accepted as a fashionable way to offer entertainment and draw the young bucks into the well-lit reception rooms where eligible young ladies might be viewed and appreciated for their potential as future brides.

Lord Edward was considered to be a most fortunate card player, for he displayed remarkable skill at the gaming tables. He always smiled and offered his fellow players a warm handshake when the games were done and he was filling his purse with his prize of gold coins.

On the final night of Cordelia's stay in London, she was sipping her glass of punch and watching the other guests in the elegant ballroom, when someone touched her bare shoulder and gently moved an artfully trailing curl of her lovely auburn hair aside.

She turned and stared into the pale grey eyes of Lord Edward Fitzhugh, and her heart nearly stopped beating.

He bowed to her, and when he looked up again he was smiling.

"Your servant, my Lady."

Miss Millpost, standing beside Cordelia, seemed on the verge of apoplexy when she noticed that the young Lord was being far too familiar with her charge, and without a formal introduction!

Cordelia, well used to Miss Millpost, was aware of her disapproval, and ignored it.

Miss Millpost would, no doubt, berate her soundly later. She was more interested in what Lord Edward had to say, than in Miss Millpost's opinion at that moment.

He looked into Cordelia's eyes and she found the intensity of his attention flattering, if almost unnerving.

"Pray, my Lady, would you grant me the boon of your favour and let me hear from your lips the sound of your name? For 'tis a perfect misery to my heart to behold your loveliness and not know how to address you."

At this rather overly dramatic pronouncement, Miss Millpost coughed so loudly that people in the vicinity turned to see if she were having a spasm, or a fit of the vapours.

"Sir!" she finally spoke with a steely edge to her voice. "You may address that question to me, for I am sure that you have not been formally introduced to the young lady and that you presume too much by speaking to her!"

The young lord laughed.

"The fault is entirely mine for forgetting my manners in the presence of such beauty. I was bewitched and enchanted by the lady's smile and I no longer know what I do."

Cordelia nearly clapped her hands in delight at his poetic manner, but managed to restrain herself beneath the watchful gaze of the disapproving Miss Millpost, who continued to speak to him firmly.

"Sirrah, I will have none of your poetry and nonsense! This is the elder daughter of the Baron Tillingford whose estates lie but two days' ride from London and whose family are well known to His Majesty the King! Who might you be, to presume so rudely to speak to her?"

Fitzhugh bowed deeply before Cordelia, with a dramatic sweep of his arm that brought his forefinger to almost touching the marble floor at the young Lady's feet, before drawing himself up to his full height and declaring, "And I am Lord Edward Fitzhugh, my Lady, and I am at your service."

Cordelia almost stuttered in the presence of the young Lord, so swept away by his looks and manner did she feel, but she made an attempt at appropriate behaviour, nonetheless.

"I am not at all certain, my Lord, that this represents a suitable introduction, to allow me to speak with you, within the bounds of propriety."

"Those foolish conventions apply only to the lesser mortals who strut but briefly upon this globe of dust and dreams. But you are divine, my Lady, a goddess, Venus herself come down from lofty Olympus to earth to torment the hearts of mere men and you have stolen both my wits and my heart, which I give to thee most gladly!"

Cordelia began to suspect that her heart would burst out of her chest as her face lit up with undisguised joy.

"I am Lady Cordelia, my Lord," she said, as she curtsied, "and I pray that I do not intrude too heavily upon your sensibilities."

"The intrusion is an oasis of perfect delight in this warren of the mediocre. Does a goddess require refreshment? More punch perhaps?"

Miss Millpost chose that moment to step purposefully between the couple.

"You have a way with words, Sirrah, and a pretty turn of phrase. Perhaps we should all go to the punch bowl to seek refreshment and ensure that the Lady's honour and reputation remain as pure and unsullied as they were when we first arrived."

With that, Miss Millpost took a firm grip on Cordelia's elbow and guided her in the direction of the long, white damasked refreshment table. She barely acknowledged the young Lord's presence, speaking only to Cordelia as they walked.

"It is insufferably warm in here and I believe a glass of punch would be most welcome to my poor dry throat."

Lord Edward took up station on the other side of Cordelia as the trio walked towards the crystal punch bowl. He waved away the servant with a brush of his hand.

"Dearest Lady, permit me."

He filled a glass with a small measure of the bright red liquid and offered it to Cordelia. As she took it in her lace-gloved hands, Edward filled a second glass to the brim and handed it to her companion.

"Your good health, Madame," he nodded at Miss Millpost as he raised his own glass in a simple toast, "and here's to your happiness and the loveliness of your eyes, Lady Cordelia."

He noticed how quickly Miss Millpost downed her punch, and quickly offered her a second.

"Thank you, Sir. I had not realised quite how thirsty one may become at these grand occasions."

By the time that Miss Millpost had consumed her third measure of punch, she was beginning to feel a little dizzy, and a little unsteady on her feet.

"Pray, child, but the heat is becoming too much for me and I fear I must sit." Cordelia helped her to an elegantly embroidered couch and eased her onto the seat where Miss Millpost promptly closed her eyes and fell soundly, but not noiselessly, asleep. Cordelia placed a cushion beneath her head for comfort and support, and the older lady began to snore softly. A small chuckle caught her attention. When she turned her head, she discovered that Lord Edward was standing behind her.

"My dear Lady. It would appear that the kind hand of Fate has cast us adrift without the restraining anchor of your companion." He smiled broadly at the young woman. "Perhaps you would care to accompany me for a while and enthral me with tales of life on your father's estate?"

They spent the next half hour standing in front of a wide fireplace, chatting to each other as the split logs crackled and the dancing flames lent their warmth and gaiety to the room. Lord Edward proved to be a most attentive listener and smiled at every nuance and detail that Cordelia shared with him.

For his part, he said very little, preferring to listen to the young heiress whilst cleverly eluding her questions with humour and evasive replies, implying that, despite his wealth and position, he really didn't take himself too seriously.

He seemed effortlessly charming, an open book, a man of wealth and position who only played cards for the fun of the sport, a man who enjoyed seeing his wealthy young friends squeal with horror whenever they lost. Which seemed to happen a lot.

A sudden and dramatic cough interrupted the young couple as Miss Millpost approached with a bleary eye and a slight waver in her gait.

"Ah! There you are, Lady Cordelia. I was resting my eyes for a moment and when I opened them again, you were gone."

Cordelia tried not to laugh.

"Yes, Miss Millpost, I saw that you were resting and I could not bring myself to disturb you. So I waited for you here by the warmth of the hearth and Lord Edward kindly volunteered to keep me company until you felt refreshed."

The companion cast a critical eye over Lord Edward and nodded her head.

"I see. Very thoughtful of the gentleman. Very thoughtful indeed. Well, we must be away. It is already late. I shall summon our carriage, for you will need your rest, if you are to be fresh for tomorrow's activities."

She turned on her heel and went to find a footman. Lord Edward murmured in Cordelia's ear, so close that she could feel the warmth of his breath upon her skin.

"She could probably outdrink half the men under service in His Majesty's Navy!" Cordelia laughed at his words, even as she felt a tingling warmth flow through her when the young Lord touched the tips of her fingers with his own. "And I would see you again, if you would permit me, sweet Lady Cordelia."

She smiled as she looked into his pale eyes.

"We leave for my home tomorrow morning, but I am sure that you would always be welcome to visit," she hesitated for a heartbeat, "for I would always be pleased to see you, Lord Edward."

Miss Millpost stepped back into the room and immediately seized the hand that she saw was far too close to the young Lord's fingertips. "Time to go, Lady Cordelia, time to go. Lord Edward, it was a pleasure meeting you. We shall take our leave and be on our way now."

"Farewell, Lord Edward," Cordelia spoke as she was half coaxed, half pulled from the room, "'til we meet again."

He bowed his head and blew a gentle kiss to her that she could've sworn had sailed across the widening gap that was opening between them and brushed against the smoothness of her beautiful cheek. She raised a gloved hand to her face in an attempt to hold the impression of the kiss upon her face for the rest of eternity.

Lady Cordelia Branley, Baron Tillingford's beautiful elder daughter, was hopelessly in love.

Chapter Three

Night had settled upon the great house as the Baron sat back in his favourite chair and felt the warmth of the fire in the library's ornate hearth.

"So, you have been presented into society and, if Cousin Mathilde is to be believed, you made a fair impression on the good people you met, my dear."

Cordelia's eyes shone with excitement as she recounted tales of the Balls, the card games and the talk amongst the elegant guests who attended the fashionable salons of London's great houses.

"And I hear that you met a young gentleman who seems to have paid you a great deal of attention."

Cordelia could not prevent herself from blushing.

"And may your old father not learn the name of this young gentleman?"

His pretty daughter giggled and looked down at her hands. "Of course you may, Papa. He is Lord Edward Fitzhugh."

The Baron nodded for a few moments and lit his fine-stemmed clay pipe. "Fitzhugh, you say?" He took a moment to draw the flame onto the tightly-packed tobacco before exhaling a plume of sweet, blue smoke. "Fitzhugh. Yes. I believe I am acquainted with his father."

Cordelia looked up at her father. "I heard that the Earl of Bolton is away in Spain, fighting the French, Papa."

"Indeed he is. For after the death of his wife last year, he could no longer bear to live amongst his memories, and chose, as his elder son and heir, George, is most capable, to leave him to manage his estates here, whilst the Earl took himself off to war. It was my belief that he had expected his second son to follow him into the Army, as most second sons with a skerrick of care for their country have done these last bitter years. Perhaps we should ask ourselves why his fit and able-bodied young son is not at his father's side, thwarting Boney's plans to take over the whole world?"

"I cannot answer that, Papa, but I'm sure that Lord Edward will be willing to offer his sword in the King's service as soon as he is needed."

The ageing aristocrat laughed.

"Needed, my dear daughter? Of a certainty, every sword and ship is needed right now!" There was a pause as the logs in the fireplace settled and sent a shower of sparks up the chimney and out into the cold, night air. "I hope he isn't one of those damnable fops who parade around London in their silken breeches with their oiled hair and foolish fashions, instead of serving their King like true men in the defence of English freedom!"

Cordelia was a little surprised at the vehemence of her father's words, for he had most always been the steadiest of men. Without waiting for her to respond, the Baron continued

"There is, that I know of, nothing to hold young Edward back. His brother George is more than competent, and well trained to take on the role of Earl should his father find death at the hands of the French. It does, truly, leave me puzzled at the young man's continued presence in London. Until you spoke of him, I had assumed that he had already followed his father to the continent."

Cordelia did not have a reply. She was sure, in her heart, that her handsome hero was probably the bravest and most gallant man in the whole land, and that he would soon make short shrift of Napoleon and his legions if he needed to draw his sword and answer the call to arms. She was absolutely sure of it. Her father however, drawing gently on his pipe in the quiet seclusion of the candlelit library, was considerably less convinced about Lord Edward Fitzhugh than his daughter.

As if by unspoken consent, neither mentioned him further, and their conversation moved on to discussion of the coming summer, and what social occasions might be found to entertain a young woman, away from the sweltering miasma of London air.

When the Baron suggested that they might remove to Quincy House in Bath for the summer, Cordelia's eyes lit up with excitement. Her thoughts immediately went to the fact that so many of the *ton* spend the summer in Bath, surely she would meet many wonderful young gentlemen there. And... maybe, Lord Edward would also be there?

The Baron smiled indulgently at his daughter's reaction.

"So be it then. We will go to Bath for the summer. I will send Garrig off tomorrow, to get the house opened up and make sure it's in order for us to arrive there in a month's time."

"Oh father! Thank you!   A summer in Bath will be wonderful!" Cordelia swept from the room, off to tell Georgiana the news.

<center>~~~~~</center>

The Baron leant back in his chair, his breath laboured, and his heart aching. For the proposed trip to Bath was not, as he had presented it, just for his daughter's benefit. His physician had recommended, just last week, that he spend some time there, and take the waters, in the hope that it would improve his health. He could not bear to tell his daughters, yet, just how poor his health had become.

He knew that, if he was honest with himself, he was not going to get better. It was only a matter of time – time in which he wished to see at least one of the girls well married and cared for, the better that both of them might cope when he died.

That thought led him back to Lord Edward Fitzhugh.

Cordelia's obvious attraction to the young Lord Edward was to be expected – she was at an age when a dashing young man could easily turn a girl's head. What concerned him more was the fact that the young man was in London at all, for Cordelia to have met him.   He had meant what he said about having believed that Lord Edward would already have taken himself off to war, following in his father's footsteps.

It did not sit well with him that the boy was still in England.

He would need to find out more, before he could be comfortable with Cordelia showing such interest in the young man. He knew just who to ask.

There were few friends who he had known for more than 20 years, and fewer now that the war had taken so many, but some remained that he trusted utterly. Of those, he was quite certain who to send to. Cecil Carlisle, Baron Setford, had been a school friend of Philip Canterwood, the Duke of Rotherhithe, and he had met them both at the same house party, all those years ago.

Rotherhithe was a well-respected figure in Parliament now, but Setford was something more complex. Setford, it seemed, had the Prince Regent's ear, but was not very publicly visible. It was the Baron's belief that the man's role was that of a spymaster for the crown, although such a thing would never, of course, be acknowledged. If anyone could discover the truth of Lord Edward Fitzhugh's continued presence in England, it would be Setford.

The Baron rose, coughing at the movement, dismayed at the small flecks of blood on his kerchief when he wiped his mouth, and went to his desk. He penned a most carefully phrased missive to Baron Setford, asking him to make some enquiries, to set an old friend at ease over the boy who had caught his daughter's interest, and inviting Setford to visit them in Bath, for a Ball and small house party which he intended to organise.

He sanded the letter and set it to dry, leaning back in his chair and savouring the rich mellow brandy that soothed his throat, considering all that he needed to do, in the time he had left.

Once the ink was dry, he folded and sealed the letter, and rang for a footman, giving instructions for it to be sent without delay, the following morning.

Chapter Four

The County of Berkshire, England – late April 1815

Four weeks after Cordelia's return from London, the Baron received a message from a courier who had ridden all the way from London.

The young man in his mud-splashed cloak delivered the letter directly into the Baron's hand and touched his cap in a gesture of respect when he received a shining silver sixpenny piece for his trouble. The Baron sent him on his way to the stables, assuring him of food and a bed before he should need to start his return journey.

"Cordelia!" The Baron's voice echoed up the grand staircase as the servants brought fresh bread, eggs, meats, coffee and sweet preserves to the dining room table for breakfast. "You will be late for your breakfast and I have news for you. And find Georgiana! I do declare the scamp is outside in the cold, playing with the puppies in the stables again!"

As his elder daughter sat down at the breakfast table and Georgiana came racing into the room with freshly scrubbed face and hands, the Baron cleared his throat and handed the letter he'd just received to Cordelia.

"You can read and eat at the same time, I trust?" he smiled, carefully concealing the small fleck of blood that had appeared at the side of his mouth.

"Who is it from, Papa?"

"Read it and see! Read it and all shall be revealed!"

The Baron covered his mouth again with the fine linen napkin and coughed, aware that more droplets of bright red blood had stained the fabric.

"Papa! My stars! It is from Lord Edward. He asks permission to visit. Is this true?"

"Who's Lord Edward?" Georgiana was busily covering a warm bread roll with butter and damson jam, managing to spill crumbs onto her puppy footprinted and mud-flecked dress in the process.

"Would you like to see the young man again, my dear?"

The Baron watched Cordelia's face – if this would make her happy, he was willing to invite the young man to stay with them in Bath, despite his concerns. He had heard nothing as yet from Setford, so he had to presume that, whatever young Fitzhugh was up to, it was not too dire.

"Who's Lord Edward?" asked Georgiana, past a mouthful of warm roll and jam.

"Of course I would, Papa. He's such a wonderful, handsome man, I'm sure you will like him."

"Who's Lord Edward?" repeated Georgiana as she took another bite of bread roll and a sip from her glass of milk.

"Then I shall accept his suggestion and invite him to attend upon us at Quincy House in Bath. But he will need to be entertained and what better excuse could we possibly have for staging a Ball? We can invite all those of quality who will be in Bath for the summer, as well as a few old friends from near here."

"Oh, Papa! I shall be the happiest girl in the country!"

"Who's Lord Edward?" said Georgiana, but it gradually dawned on her that, amongst all the excited chatter at the breakfast table, no one was really listening to her. She looked at her half-eaten roll and whispered to it "Who's Lord Edward?" with frustration evident in her tone.

~~~~~

The courier was sent back to London with a reply, inviting Lord Edward Fitzhugh to attend upon Baron Tillingford at Quincy House in Bath, for a grand Ball and house party, to be held in the second week of May.

A stream of other missives were sent from Casterfield Grange that morning, to the house in Bath, informing the staff of the planned activities, and to a remarkably large number of persons, who 'just had to be invited' to the Ball. The Baron found it amusing, if a little exhausting.
~~~~~

If he was to die soon, he might as well host a grand entertainment first. His daughters deserved it. He had not hosted a Ball or house party since his wife's death – a fact which would guarantee good attendance, even if only so that the *ton* could satisfy their curiosity about him, and his family.

Chapter Five

Lord Edward Fitzhugh had proposed a visit to his father's old acquaintance on the entirely spurious grounds that he felt he was obliged to pay the Baron his respects whilst his father the Earl was unavoidably detained in Spain. It was only good manners.

The young Lord suggested that he might provide better company during the visit if he could bring a group of friends along and the Baron agreed, not without some minor concern. Still, better to see what these young men of the *ton* were like, in his own house, than to wonder. Having committed himself to the endeavour of hosting a grand social occasion, he might as well make it something to be remembered.

He muttered to himself, as he penned the response, in the positive, to the young Lord's request.

"It's about time we had some young blood in the house instead of these old bones rattling around like a gathering of ghosts!"

It was unfortunate that the Baron had chosen that precise moment to cast his gaze upon Miss Millpost, as she entered the room with Cordelia and Georgiana. Miss Millpost, also unfortunately, heard his mutterings and promptly felt most righteously offended to be classed with the Baron as a bag of old bones - or even as a ghost - obviously on account of her maturity. She had sniffed and drawn herself up to her full height to declare that was she was still very much in the prime of her life.

The Baron had clearly not intended to slight the companion and he calmed her indignation with the peace offering of a generous glass of Madeira. And then another. And order and good grace were soon restored to the Baron's household whilst Cordelia and Georgiana giggled uncontrollably behind Miss Millpost's rigidly unbending back.

<center>~~~~~</center>

The remove of the household to Bath would happen in the last week of April. All was planned, but last minute arrangements had everyone rushing about frenetically, sure that something was being forgotten.

Cordelia's excitement was mounting, and the wait until she would see Lord Edward again seemed interminable. At random intervals, she would simply stop, in the midst of packing, with a dress clasped to her as she imagined lord Edward seeing her in it, or with a look of indecision as she wondered which necklace he might like best when she wore it.

Georgiana was, whilst interested to see this paragon that her sister spoke of in such glowing terms, somewhat cynical.

She had yet to meet a fashionable man that she considered worth bothering about. And she wasn't at all sure that she wished to behave 'like a grown up young Lady should' as that seemed to involve no playing with puppies, no visits to the stables, no mess, and generally no fun. At fifteen, she was well aware of what society might expect of her, but she wasn't the least bit interested in fulfilling those expectations, yet, at least.

The fact that her sister seemed to have become a ninnyhammer who spent half her day woolgathering, just because she had met some young Lord, simply confirmed her low opinion of the whole 'being a proper young Lady' process.

Eventually, despite everyone's fears, everything was packed, and three coaches, with staff, family, and possessions set off for the trip to Bath. They travelled slowly, taking two days to cover the distance, for everyone's better comfort. Georgiana found the travel more interesting than all of the preparations, watching with fascination the coming and going at the Inn where they stopped overnight, as the ostlers dealt with an enormous number of horses and carriages, all without any issues or argument.

Cordelia simply found the entire process wearing – she wanted to be in Bath now, she wanted it to be next week, and for Lord Edward to have arrived. Everything else was unimportant to her…. Well, maybe except the Ball – that was still exciting!

Upon arrival at Quincy House, the chaos happened all over again, with the unpacking, and rushing from room to room exploring and exclaiming. The girls had not been to Quincy House for many years, so everything seemed new to them.

Their last visit had been when they were small children, and the house had still been exactly as it was when Great Aunt Petrina had still been alive – long before their birth. The ancient furniture and old fashioned dark panelling with dark wallpaper had made it a gloomy place for children. Now, in the weeks since they had decided to come here, the staff had worked miracles, and the house was transformed.

Cordelia was ecstatic, and wanted to be involved in every part of the arrangements for the Ball. Georgiana considered her insane to wish so, but looked on her with a sister's puzzled patience – a patience which was much better maintained when Georgiana spent most of her time exploring the extensive garden, the stables and the attics. Attics which appeared to contain a few generations worth of intriguing stored items, as well as enough dust to drive the maids to despair, when she returned with it liberally attached to her clothes.

And so it went for the two weeks between their arrival and the Ball and house party – Cordelia dreamed of love and poetry, and dark hair and grey eyes, whilst Georgiana escaped the planning and indulged her imagination anywhere she could hide.

Chapter Six

The Ball required an enormous amount of organisation, rather more than the Baron seemed to remember from Balls when his wife was alive. He had to conclude that she had been far more skilled at all of this than he had realised at the time.

Musicians had to be hired. Fine plate and crystal glasses needed to be washed and polished to a shine. Food, wine, tobacco and provisions had to be prepared. Candles and oil lamps needed to be trimmed and prepared in great quantity to allow all of the chandeliers in the ballroom to be lit. Clothes needed to be brushed and pressed and bed linen for the guests brought out of storage.

It should have required a whole month, he realised, but, somehow, it was done in the two weeks that were available before the date he had set. The house looked wonderful as the sunshine warmed the earth and the green shoots which spring had brought forth grew into an abundance of life returning to the fields and hedgerows as summer began.

The Baron had invited all of the local dignitaries to the Ball, as well as those of the ton who had taken up residence in Bath for the summer, and old friends like Philip Canterwood, Duke of Rotherhithe. The Duke was eight years younger than the Baron, a strong and healthy man in the prime of life, and reputed to be fabulously wealthy. He was a man whose advice the Prince Regent respected, and whose service in Parliament was lauded. He was also a dogged supporter of the war against Napoleon.

The Baron sincerely hoped that the Duke would grace the Ball with his presence. It would certainly add an additional measure of prestige to the occasion, but, more than that, the Baron was looking forward to seeing his old friend again.

In truth, he was very fond of the Duke. At this stage in his life and with his health all too rapidly deteriorating, the Baron had few friends left in the world that he could call on, for so many had been lost to war. He was thoroughly delighted when he received word that the Duke would be most pleased to attend the Ball and that he was looking forward to raising a rousing toast to the Baron's health and happiness and long life. Those lines in the Duke's letter brought a wry smile to the Baron's face, for he was quite certain that his life would not be long, or healthy, although perhaps happiness was not too much to ask.

The preparations progressed smoothly, apart from the occasional interference from Miss Millpost who, in the absence of the Baron's still sorely-missed wife, often presumed to assume the role of the female head of the household. This did little to make her popular with the servants and brought an inevitable gentle rebuke from the Baron who appreciated her kindness and efforts but not her presumption.

He would calm her with a glass of Madeira in the library and urge her to leave the arrangements to his loyal and experienced staff.

Clearly, she would have loved nothing more than to assume the title of mistress of the great house, but that was a fantasy that would never be fulfilled.

With his health as it was, the Baron had no intention of re-marrying, any more than he had had from the time of his wife's death, and, if he had been forced to choose a bride at his time of life, he would undoubtedly have sought a titled lady with spirit and vitality, a lady who would have brought joy and laughter into the household, in contrast to Miss Millpost's grim and notorious sense of discipline and propriety.

And yet the preparations progressed in an orderly and timely fashion and the Baron was pleased with the lovely decorations that filled the elegant and under-used ballroom. He fondly remembered the brightly-lit Balls that his young wife had enjoyed so much, the hundreds of flickering candles, the glittering chandeliers, the laughter and chatter, the music and dancing, the wonderful array of dishes and the excellent wines.

There had been no occasions on which he could face the idea of holding a Ball in his household since his dearly beloved wife had passed away, but the thought of his lovely daughter, hopefully, acquiring a suitor at the tender age of seventeen made him smile. A grand excuse to hold a Ball!

But there would be no rush, of course. Everything would proceed at a genteel and carefully measured pace.

He did not wish to see Cordelia married too soon, yet there may be no choice, and he prayed that he would live long enough to escort her down the isle of the parish church on her wedding day. It was, in many ways, his fondest wish.

Chapter Seven

Baron Tillingford's guests began to arrive at the stately house two full days before the Ball was due to be held.

At eleven in the morning (remarkably early for the *ton*), two fine carriages drew up at the front of Quincey House – one rather more elegant and imposing than the other. From the richly appointed first coach an elegantly attired man in a dark blue cloak and immaculately polished riding boots stepped out, without waiting for the carriage step to be lowered.

He was tall, with a finely edged jaw and prominent well-shaped nose and he looked up at the great house with a smile. Philip Canterwood, Duke of Rotherhithe, settled his fashionable hat upon his thick dark hair, where the streaks of grey at his temple simply emphasised the wisdom that age had provided and lent a patrician dignity to his appearance. A well put together man in his early forties, he presented a handsome picture, with none of the foppish excess that so many young men of the day displayed.

From the second carriage, which was of no lesser quality, yet presented an understated elegance of appearance, with no crest or distinguishing marks visible, descended a gentleman somewhat less striking in appearance, but who was obviously a man of the nobility.

Cecil Carlisle, Baron Setford, was not one for ostentation. His clothing was of the best quality, simply cut by the best tailors, his hair a mid-brown, and his eyes a piercing light grey. Were it not for his eyes, one might pass him by on the street, barely noticing him. The eyes arrested one's attention, showing a sharp intelligence and an interest in every detail of his surroundings.

The great doors swung open and the Baron hurried down the steps to greet each of his old friends with a firm handshake and a hand on the shoulder.

~~~~~

Cordelia, peeking through the parlour window, was unable to contain her excitement, for these first arrivals meant that the house party had truly begun, and the grand Ball was not far off!

She was struck by the first gentleman's appearance – he was handsome, and projected an aura of quiet power that was attractive. He was a little older than the men that she generally found attractive, but there was something about him, something that drew her, appealed to her. She shook her head at her whimsy. How could she even consider another man worth looking at, when, soon, Lord Edward would be here!

She barely noted the second gentleman at all.
~~~~~

Moments later, as the men entered the house, Cordelia, quickly left the room – she did not want to be seen to be peeping out the window like a child – even if that was exactly what she was doing!

~~~~

They left the footmen to unload the Duke and Baron Setford's luggage. For such a short visit, the Duke seemed to have packed for a month. Baron Setford's luggage appeared to be of a somewhat more modest scale. Once initial greetings were done with, the three men settled into the deep wing back chairs in the library, with glasses of rich golden brandy,

"Canterwood, my dear friend. How good it is to see you after all these years."

"Tillingford, you look like you've been arm-wrestling with the angel of death! What in the Lord's name ails thee?"

Blunt as ever, and never excessively renowned for his diplomatic skills (except in critical situations), the Duke was valued by the crown, and by the government he served, for his brutal honesty and his candid views. He had never seen the value in sugaring the pill. It had certainly made him enemies. It had also gained him the respect of the King, then the Prince Regent, and the Prime Minister. Especially in a time of war.

"Ah, Canterwood. Nothing escapes your attention, does it, my friend?"

Setford chuckled at Baron Tillingford's rather ironic tone, and added his own comment.
~~~~

"Damnably obvious that you're not well, Tillingford. Question is – what are you doing about it?"

"I have been diagnosed with the consumption."

Tillingford's tone was grave. He turned towards the Duke and continued.

"Though I have managed to keep it a secret from the children and from the household, they will know the truth of it soon enough, my dear friends."

"You should've taken another wife. Not natural to live alone with no female comfort. No wonder you contracted the illness. Sleeping alone, I'll wager, in a damp bed. Recipe for ill health if ever there was one!"

"I could never remarry, Canterwood." The Baron shook his head sadly. "My wife was irreplaceable. It would feel like an offense to her memory to marry again. Never found a woman who could tempt me to it."

The Duke snorted. "Then what about a serving girl, eh? Plenty of them running about on the estate. Something to keep your old bones warm at night? What's wrong with that for pity's sake? Even I, although I've not been able to bring myself to re-marry after Angeline and the babe's death, must admit to having taken comfort where I find it in the years since. Surely you could do the same?"

Setford nodded agreement, watching Tillingford's face.

Tillingford chuckled and shook his head again.

"I think not, Canterwood. Not even for the sake of my health, bad though that is!"

A cough interrupted his speech, and the other men waited patiently for him to go on.

"And heaven knows what the parson would say if he ever found out I'd taken advantage of a maid – after all, I've made a point of not being like so many of the nobility – wouldn't want to disappoint him now! No, my friend. I sleep with my memories and they are enough for me. My real fear is that the consumption will take me before Cordelia is married."

The two men before him nodded, their expressions sober.

"If anything happened to me, I do not know what would happen to my daughters. After all – I have no heir, and, to the best of my knowledge, there are no male heirs in the bloodline, not even distant ones. I fear that, after 800 years, the Barony of Tillingford will no longer be held by a Branley. It may, in fact, cease to exist completely, dependent upon the whim of the Prince Regent. It's a troubling thought."

The Duke leaned forward and put a firm hand on the Baron's knee.

"If anything happens to you, my dear Tillingford, you may look to me to take care of your daughters."

The Baron looked at his friend, only 8 years his junior, yet still strong, robust and full of vigour and he knew that salvation was at hand. How he envied the man his health and strength in that moment.

"My dear Canterwood, you have just removed a great weight from my mind. I cannot thank you enough for your offer."

To his surprise, Tillingford found himself at the edge of tears. He had not, until that moment, realised just how heavy a weight of worry he was carrying.

"Are you alright, Tillingford?" asked the Duke.

"Oh, yes," replied the Baron, feeling a tightness in his throat as the emotion rose in his chest, and he wiped his eye. "It's just a mote of dust from the fire. A mote of dust. Nothing more."

After a moment, Setford spoke quietly.

"Are all your properties entailed, old man? Are you able to settle anything substantial on your daughters?"

Tillingford smiled.

"That, at least, is not a problem. Fully half of my estates are not entailed, including this fine house, and Casterfield Grange, which has been our permanent home since my wife's passing. I have money enough for a fine dowry for both girls, and property to settle upon them at my death. My man of business has all of the papers in readiness. I have no intention of dying without doing my best to provide for their futures."

Setford and the Duke nodded, glad that Tillingford was so pragmatic, and well prepared. Setford appeared deep in thought for a while as they sat back in their comfortable chairs and sipped their brandy in silence, while the log fire cast its warmth into the room and memories stirred in the hearts of the three men. Eventually Setford spoke again.

"Old friend, I can see that the fate of the Barony weighs heavily on you – for I know that you have always been a good steward of the land, and done well by your tenants. Are you quite certain that no male heir exists?"

"Quite – I've had Benson and Sons searching for years now. To no avail. You are right – the thought that the estates might pass to someone who would run them down, and abuse the tenants, worries me deeply."

At the mention of the renowned legal firm, Setford paused. If Benson's couldn't trace an heir, there was likely none. He had known Benson for years, and, at times, used their discreet services. The crack of a log in the fireplace broke the silence, and sparks drifted on the hearth. Setford sat, staring into the flames, his fingers occasionally drumming on the chair arm. He sipped his brandy, then appeared to come to a decision.

"Tillingford, I can make no promises, you understand... but... I do have the Prince Regent's ear at times. I believe that I know of a young man, good, solid, respectable, currently doing more than sterling service for his country in Spain, in a greatly difficult role. A man who, if he manages to survive the next months at war, might find the Prince Regent wishing to reward him, in some very substantial way. He is a man that I am quite certain would do full honour to the name and history of the Barony, should he be granted its care and title. I will undertake, should no male heir be found, to influence things in that direction, when the time comes."

The Duke looked at Setford with interest.

"I had understood, old friend, that your endeavours in recent years had brought you close to the Prince Regent, and to some of the more undercover aspects of the war. It seems that I am correct in that understanding. And grateful for it in this circumstance. Should there be anything I can do to assist you with this, I will be only too happy to oblige."

Baron Tillingford looked at the men before him, men he had known and respected for more than 20 years, and was deeply grateful for having them as friends.

His heart felt lighter for the conversation, no matter how depressing talking of one's own forthcoming death was, and he breathed easier knowing that someone else shared his cares.

"I thank you both. It is a great relief to me, to know that someone else will care about the fate of my title and lands, as well as that of my daughters. And, speaking of my daughters, I must ask, Setford, if you have any information for me, about the doings of that young popinjay that Cordelia seems to have conceived an affection for."

Setford laughed lightly, breaking the sombre tone of the discussion.

"Popinjay indeed! A good description for the boy. I've been delving a bit into his habits and friends. Nothing specifically wrong that I've found, but I agree with you, it's very odd that he's not gone off to war after his father. Smacks of disrespect. His brother George doesn't seem to have much time for him either. George is a good sort, manages the estates well – he'll make a good Earl for Bolton when his father's gone."

The Duke looked at Tillingford for a moment, absorbing what Setford had said, then spoke.

"Bolton's boy, you say?" He stroked his clean-shaven chin and drew on his pipe of sweet Virginia twist. "I know the Earl well enough. Fine fellow. Good man. Wellesley speaks highly of him. But I do not know either son." He paused to sip from his brandy.

"I am, however, in agreement with you it is odd that the boy has not done his patriotic duty and bought a commission – I am most curious to learn why the young shaver is not serving King and country with his father against the blasted French in Spain."

Tillingford nodded.

"That is why I asked Setford to look into it, quietly. I have not, myself, yet spoken to Fitzhugh about the matter and I did not wish to upset my daughter who is clearly infatuated with him. Yet, in truth my dear Canterwood, from Miss Millpost's report of what she saw in London, he seems remarkably evasive when confronted with a direct and simple question on the topic."

Setford nodded and continued with his commentary.

"Edward is another matter entirely from his brother. Spends his days with other young fribbles, delights in the cards, and always seems to win. A little too often, if you ask me, although I've nothing to say it's not just luck. Always seems to have money to burn too, and I've not uncovered any hidden debts… yet. Still, all in all, I don't like the feel of it. So, for now, I'd say it's a watching brief."

"Ah, that does not reassure me, my friend, not at all. We shall see how he behaves over the next week, he and his friends, and hope that my daughter sees sense, instead of continuing to harbour a *tendre* for him."

<center>~~~~~</center>

Also amongst the first to arrive, but a few hours after the Duke and Setford, was the dashing Lord Edward Fitzhugh and his three titled companions.

Their coach was drawn by four matched blacks and lavishly decorated within and without. The carriage doors bore the Earl of Bolton's coat of arms and the coachman and guard wore the Earl's distinctive green and gold livery.

The vehicle was as comfortable as the skilled craftsmen and coach-builders could possibly make it, with over-stuffed, padded leather seating and an inlaid ebony case in the centre of the floor that securely held both wine and crystal glasses and spirits for the passengers' pleasure and comfort. It was a marvel of the age and had cost the Earl a small fortune to commission and build – a fortune he had spent for his wife's benefit.

Upon her death, he had asked that the coach be stored away, and refused to use it himself.

But the Earl was with the King's army in faraway Spain, fighting the forces of Napoleon, and his son had thought it a waste and a sacrilege to leave such a fine and handsome carriage unused in a humble stable block on his father's extensive estate. He'd ordered the coach brought to London for his personal use and its polished and painted woodwork soon became a regular sight on the capital's streets as it conveyed Edward and his companions to the fashionable salons and drawing rooms where he loved to play cards.

The Baron smiled as he stood at the top of the wide stone staircase to welcome his guests. He extended a firm handshake to young Lord Edward and introduced himself with a polite nod of the head.

Edward's manners were impeccable and he exerted his charm on the elderly Baron, complimenting his host on the elegance of the great house.

It was impossible not to find the young man pleasing, as he moved with studied poise and grace, lifting his chin to toss his oiled and coiffed curls and smiling at all and everyone.

Even at Miss Millpost, to whom he extended an exaggerated and courtly bow as if he were in the presence of an empress. She appeared slightly less convinced of the young man's sincerity than the rest of the staff.

The gossip below stairs talked of little else other than engagements and weddings and a match made in heaven. Cordelia agonised in her chamber over which dress to wear that evening, when she would meet Lord Edward again after two whole months' separation.

She had thought of precious little else. He occupied all of her waking thoughts and feelings, and had taken full possession of her heart without the slightest hint of resistance. She was seventeen and everyone with eyes to see could tell that the young Lady Cordelia Branley was head over heels in love with Lord Edward Fitzhugh.

One glimpse of his dashing smile and refined manners, and everyone could understand why. Everyone, perhaps, except for Cordelia's younger sister, the energetic Georgiana.

She watched the young Lord with wide eyes as he bowed and made elegant flourishes with his scented kerchief to underline his words, and could not for one moment begin to understand what all the fuss was about. Cook laughed when Georgiana (who was in the kitchen in search of biscuits for an afternoon snack) explained that Edward seemed to her to be a great deal of fuss over nothing.

"You'll think differently when you're a little older, my poppet!"

Georgiana had looked up at the plump cook and declared in a solemn voice, "Why, I hope I have much more sense than that," and the entire kitchen staff had roared with laughter.

At that, Georgiana had turned up her nose in a huff, and gone to spend the rest of the afternoon in the stables. They might be smaller than the stables at Casterfield Grange, but the grooms who had come with them knew her, and, anyway, there were kittens, tucked away in the straw in the loft. She hoped that she would never be so air-headed as Cordelia was being, all because of a handsome man.

~~~~~

Her equilibrium restored by her afternoon in the stables, Georgiana had rushed into her sister's chambers to see if she had finally chosen a gown for the evening, and then stated, in innocent sincerity, that she thought absolutely any dress would be suitable because Cordelia was so beautiful that she could wear anything. Cordelia smiled at the compliment, beaming joyfully at her little sister.

"And what do you think of Lord Edward, Georgiana? Is he not the most handsome man you have ever seen?"

Georgiana was not particularly gifted in the art of diplomacy and could no more lie to her beloved sister than sprout wings and fly.

"He reminds me of a story that Papa read to us."
~~~~~

"A story, you say? Of gallant knights rescuing fair damsels from captivity and slaying dragons to save the kingdom?"

"Not really." She pursed her lips in concentration. "I was thinking more of the story of the clever monkey that learned to walk on two legs and talk and ape the manners of gentle folk."

There was a hushed silence in the bedchamber. Cordelia slowly drew in her breath. Then Georgiana smiled.

"But he became very famous and met the king because a talking monkey was such a funny thing that everyone in the whole wide kingdom wanted one as a pet."

With a laugh, and an impish smile, she turned lightly on her heel and ran out of the room, happy to have shared her views and confidently not expecting her sister to take any offence at her words. The chambermaid shook her head, tutted and laughed.

"She is still but a child, Your Ladyship, even though she has just turned sixteen this past week, she might as well still be thirteen, for all that she notices men. Children know no better at that age, and care not at all, until the day that they look at a man and see more than a nuisance. I seem to remember that you were not so different..."

Cordelia sighed.

"I believe you are right, Mary. She knows no better and we should be patient with her. But, in faith, to compare Lord Edward to an ape! That is most unfair and an outrage, no mistake."

Chapter Eight

Baron Tillingford had ordered the kitchen staff to prepare a supper with a fine selection of wines to welcome the first of his guests that evening. A log fire warmed the dining room and the conversation touched on the war with France, the shortages of French wine that had been occasioned by the Royal navy's blockade of Bonaparte's ports, the state of the government and the health of the king.

~~~~~

When the Duke first entered the room, he had, as was his habit, looked at all of those present, assessing and considering the possible conversation. As introductions were performed, and he bowed over the hands of Tillingford's daughters, he found himself struck by Lady Cordelia. There was something about her, with her pale glowing skin and rich dark hair, she was undoubtedly beautiful, and unaware of just how much so.

Something about her seemed familiar, it nagged at his memory. He hated not remembering things.
~~~~~

It would come to him, he was sure. He would simply watch her, as the evening word on – surely something in her manner would bring to mind the reason that she seemed so familiar.

~~~~~

Cordelia sat quietly, trying not to stare at Lord Edward, deeply self-conscious about her appearance and fearful that the mist green satin gown might not be to his liking. She ate sparingly, butterflies springing up and taking riotous flight in her stomach.

Edward displayed his wit and cleverness with words, making puns and playful expressions that kept the table amused until the pudding had been served and consumed.

"Friends," said the Baron, "let us adjourn to the drawing room and perhaps persuade the more musically-inclined to offer us the benefit of their gifts."

The dozen or so guests applauded the Baron's suggestion and retired to the comfortable drawing room where Cordelia was requested to play and sing for them. Blushing and with a degree of reluctance, she took her place at the pianoforte and closed her eyes for a moment to gather her thoughts. The room became silent as she lifted her delicate fingers above the keyboard and began to play.

An accomplished pianist, with her mother's pure and lucid voice, she enchanted the company with a gentle song about two young lovers who were, in every verse, separated by their sworn duty, and the guests joined in with the lilting chorus that cast a melancholy air over the candlelit room.
~~~~~

Cordelia's father stood to applaud his daughter's beautiful playing, beaming with pride at her performance, moved by the lilt of her voice and his memories of her mother's enchanting power to hold a room with a simple tune, and then he demanded something more jolly to lift their spirits. Cordelia smiled and launched into a rousing country song that everyone knew, and soon enough even the servants and footmen were joining in with the merry chorus and the room was filled with cheering voices and stamping feet, laughter and gaiety, smiles and applause.

After that, Cordelia excused herself from the pianoforte with a small curtsy, and the Baron asked for a volunteer to raise the roof and dazzle the assembly with more singing and playing. Lord Edward's friends made a great play of trying to persuade him to take his seat at the pianoforte and, despite his protests that he possessed only the most pitiable and meagre talents as a musician, he finally, reluctantly, agreed to offer what he could.

But, he declared, on the strict condition that they all refrain from throwing rotten fruit and vegetables at him! He smiled at Cordelia as he took his seat and her heart nearly leapt out of her chest.

He cocked his head for a moment as if in thought and then he announced to the room that he would like first to offer an instrumental piece for their amusement, a tune that did not involve the use of his coarse and untrained cowherd's voice! The guests laughed good-naturedly but could not possibly know what was to follow.

Edward adjusted his lace cuffs and began to play. His command of the pianoforte was simply breath-taking. He played one of the most complex and demanding pieces anyone in the room had ever heard and he played with a fluency and sensitivity that brought tears to Cordelia's eyes. It was one of the most moving performances that any of them had ever witnessed. At the close of the piece, Edward closed his eyes for a moment in the silence that followed and then stood up and bowed formally to the other guests before again taking his seat, and beginning a song that took their breath away.

He played a ballad, and sang with a beautifully measured baritone that made the guests shake their heads in wonder. He was truly gifted. He was a prodigy. He played and sang as if the ancient classical gods of music had taken possession of his mortal frame and endowed him with the gifts of Apollo. Even the Baron was moved by the beauty of the performance. As he brought the piece to an end, he laughed out loud and immediately launched into a rousing song that had the guests clapping their hands in time to the rhythm and shouting their way through the chorus.

It was a wonderful way to while away the evening and the footmen charged the guests' crystal glasses with fine ports and sherries, as well as offering Miss Millpost her favourite Madeira.

~~~~~

The Duke barely watched the performance – he was, instead, watching Lady Cordelia, who was, quite obviously, thoroughly enamoured of the young man.
~~~~~

In the end, it was her expression as she watched Lord Edward that brought to his mind where he had seen her before. There had been one evening in London, some months before, at Lady Wellport's soiree, when he had, after a most satisfying game of cards, watched a young Lady as she was captivated by the antics of an extravagantly dressed young fop at the card tables.

Of a certainty, it had been Lady Cordelia he had watched that night. She was, now that he saw her again, no less attractive – more so, in fact. He felt an odd need to know more about her – not just that she was Tillingford's child, but what she thought about the world, what she did to amuse herself, and other minutiae like that. As he had that evening in London, he shook his head at his whimsy, and turned his attention back to the performance, as the talented young man finished playing.

~~~~~

Baron Setford watched the performance with an appreciation for more than the music – he freely admitted that the young Lord was musically gifted, more so than the average young man or woman, but it seemed to him that the evening's performance also demonstrated other gifts. The boy appeared to be rather a master at playing to an audience, at manipulating the responses of those around him, to suit his own desires.

Currently, it seemed, his desire was to set everyone at ease, to be seen as everyone's friend – a harmless and charming young man to enjoy a few days company with.

Setford thought that he was overdoing it somewhat.
~~~~~

Many years of training men for undercover work had given him a sixth sense about it. This boy just seemed entirely too smooth. Even the best of men did not get on with everyone. Hopefully, a messenger would arrive tomorrow. He wanted but one more report from his sources, to have all of the information possible about young Lord Edward. Perhaps that missive would throw better light on what was behind the boy's shining surface.

<center>~~~~~</center>

As the evening drew to a close and the Baron rose to thank his guests, he coughed a little and quickly covered his mouth to conceal the small flecks of blood that spilled from his lips, excusing himself for the hint of port that he claimed to have gone down the wrong way! It had been an entirely pleasing and satisfactory evening and bode well for the Ball that was arranged for the following night. With a courtly bow to the room, the Baron took his leave, his kerchief pressed firmly to his lips and a cough shaking his chest, whilst Cordelia lingered by the fireplace in the hope that she might be favoured with a few minutes of Lord Edward's time.

He was standing with his coterie of friends, laughing and basking in their admiration, his oiled and curled blue-black hair shining in the candlelight, when he turned and smiled at Cordelia. She raised a hand to her throat as he inclined his head and walked over to the fireplace to stand next to her.

"Lady Cordelia, you have deceived us all most cruelly by hiding your talents from the world and never once mentioning that you play and sing like an angel. Pray, how do you explain such an oversight?"

She blushed from the tips of her fingers to the tip of her pretty nose.

"Why, Sir, tis you who plays and sings most divinely." She looked down at the toes of her satin shoes and whispered. "You are indeed a wonder."

He waved the compliment away with a gentle toss of his lace kerchief and laughed.

"I would sooner listen to you than any other, Lady Cordelia, for you most surely do the greater honour to the pianoforte and your voice is a silk-spun gift from the heavens above. But tell me, are you absolutely sure you did not bewitch an angel and steal away their voice that you may charm the breasts of unwitting and mortal men?"

Cordelia laughed at the elegant compliment and looked up into Lord Edward's pale grey eyes. "Pray tell, my Lord, where did you learn to play and sing with such beauty and grace."

Lord Edward smiled, his gaze holding Cordelia, and her heart beat harder in her chest, so loudly that she was certain he would hear it.

His voice was a soft caress when he spoke.

"Ah, my dear Lady, but I must confess that I sold my soul to a wily imp for a portion of the Devil's musical craft, and now I am cursed for all eternity to wander the earth, and to forever be denied the warmth of a woman's gentle and restorative love."

"Would the love of a woman serve to restore you and rescue you from this most diabolical spell, my good Lord?"

"Oh, yes. Oh, yes, indeed. But where under heaven's great skies may I ever find such a love, Lady Cordelia? For surely am I a lost soul without it."

"You do not need to look any further, my Lord, for I would happily rescue you from this abomination with my own true love and release you forever from the terrible curse that binds you."

Edward smiled as he stepped closer. They were alone on that side of the room, the other guests settled around a chess table to one side, and involved in their own conversation.

"And would you seal the bargain of my liberty with a kiss, sweet enchantress?"

She closed her eyes and nodded her assent as Edward drew nearer and, with infinite care, brushed the outline of her lips with his own.

"Tis done, my Lady. I am now freed from my curse and I owe my life to thee and the gentleness of those beautiful lips."

Cordelia thought that her heart had stopped. An electric tingle ran down her spine and she wondered if time had stopped completely. Slowly, she opened her eyes and Edward was standing there, looking at her with a hint of mischief and a devilish grin.

"My beautiful Lady Enchantress, if my curse should prove more stubborn than we had both supposed, would you deign to offer the remedy of your lips again, should the need arise?"

"Willingly and gladly, my Lord." She smiled from the soles of her feet to the crown of rich dark hair on her head. "Willingly and gladly."

Chapter Nine

It was a miracle that Cordelia was able to find sleep at all that night, after having her passions aroused in a simple game of wit and playfulness with Lord Edward. She was utterly enthralled by his charm, his looks and his extraordinary talent as a musician. Childish tales of imps and curses had only made their encounter more exciting, more thrilling, especially knowing that such a kiss was forbidden, yet he had kissed her with others but paces away! She found it all irresistible.

With great effort, she pulled the embroidered blanket up to her chin and closed her eyes in the hope that she would dream of the young Lord. Much to her disappointment, she did not dream, and she felt she had slumbered for barely a few minutes when Georgiana burst into her bedchamber to announce that breakfast was being served, and that Cordelia was a slug-a-bed for not rising sooner.

It was morning, the sun was already up and the day of the Ball had finally arrived.

~~~~~

Throughout the early summer afternoon, a succession of carriages brought guests to the great house and servants busied themselves with coats and hats, and offered, in the drawing room, warming silver cups of spiced punch to revive the travellers. There was laughter and merriment as the visitors renewed old acquaintanceships and offered their respects to their smiling host and, with a greater deal of restraint, to the Duke.

Curious eyes followed Baron Setford, who was not often seen about in society, as the *ton* wondered how Baron Tillingford had drawn him out.

The Ball began with a delightful range of drinks and a refreshment table to one side, laden to capacity with roast meats and a dazzling array of delicacies and confectionary, to ensure that, throughout the evening, no guest would go hungry. The Baron had access to a prestigious wine merchant in London who, despite the Royal Navy's blockade of French ports, mysteriously managed to acquire a regular supply of excellent Burgundy wines.

The guests expressed their approval in a series of rousing toasts and some of the gentlemen showed evidence of the effects of a surfeit of wine quite early in the evening. Servants had prepared couches in an adjacent parlour for those guests who required some time to recover from an overindulgence – in wine, or in energetic dancing. But most of the guests were more sparing in their imbibing, and enjoyed the feast and the wine without impinging too greatly upon their sobriety.
~~~~~

Including Miss Millpost, who had decided that she would not let Cordelia out of her sight, for fear that young Lord Edward might behave in a thoroughly inappropriate manner.

After their conversation the previous afternoon, when the Baron had explained to the Duke the reason for his decision to host the Ball, and his concerns about Lord Edward, he was confident that the elegant nobleman would cast a critical eye over the young and dashing suitor who was showing such a romantic interest in his lovely daughter.

Standing quietly to one side of the room, watching as his guests gathered to dance a country dance, in a swirl of colour and energetic movement, Baron Tillingford reminded the Duke and Setford of his concerns. The Duke's response was immediate, and comforting.

"Do not worry yourself, my friend. I'll have the measure of the man soon enough, and then we'll see what he's made of."

<p style="text-align:center">~~~~~</p>

In truth, it was no hardship for the Duke to watch Lady Cordelia, keeping an eye out for her welfare. He found her a most pleasant sight, quite thoroughly enchanting. She was young, and currently infatuated, but seemed, otherwise, to be a talented, intelligent and modest young woman. He should, he realised, have expected nothing less, for Tillingford's wife had been all that, and Tillingford was a sensible chap.

She drew his eye, her gown a rich fuchsia shade unusual for a young woman – yet it suited her – she carried it well, and it made her dark hair and soft glowing skin all the more beautiful.

He resolved to dance with her, to see if he could draw her out into a little conversation while he did so. Perhaps he would even be a little scandalous, and see if he could manage to capture her for a waltz – which would, after all, present a much better opportunity for conversation! It was, he realised with a start, a very long time since he had danced, and even longer since he had considered the idea with pleasure. This was turning into a much more interesting house party than he had expected.

He moved quietly in her direction, intent upon adding his name to her dance card as soon as possible.

~~~~~

The musicians had fortified their spirits and lubricated their repertoire with a constant flow of warm punch, ably assisted by the serving girls who kept their glasses charged, and revived their spirits with stronger vintages as the evening wore on. The ballroom was bathed in the flickering light of a thousand candles and the ladies' jewellery sparkled as they twirled and dipped and followed the intricate patterns of the latest dances.

As a beautiful and dainty dance partner, Cordelia proved to be very popular with all of the gentlemen in attendance who vied for her attention and then pretended to be heartbroken when another gallant took her hand and swept her across the polished dance floor. They were all, however, most careful to stand by propriety, and only dance one dance each with her. Her dance card was full within a very short time, and she was flushed with excitement at being so much the centre of attention.
~~~~~

She was especially flattered when the Duke sought her out to claim a dance, boldly writing his name against the first designated waltz of the evening. Close up, he was as imposing as he had looked from a distance, and the warmth of his touch as he kissed her hand made her cheeks flush prettily. His intense eyes, the rich golden brown of brandy, held hers, and his smile simply emphasised the handsome lines of his face. He was elegance personified, in an understated and powerful way. For a moment, looking at him, she quite forgot about Lord Edward.

Lord Edward was as accomplished a dancer as he was a musician it seemed, a dandy on the floor in his high-waisted black velvet tail coat, adorned with gold buttons that bore his family crest. His silk waistcoat shone in the candlelight and he moved with grace and assurance, aware that all eyes were upon him as he demonstrated his mastery of the most fashionable dance steps, delighting each of the ladies he danced with.

Yet the Duke, for all his air of austerity, was a fine dancer too. Less dramatic than Edward, perhaps, more formal and less flamboyant, yet polished in his skill and utterly confident, Cordelia found herself watching him as he danced with others, almost as much as she was watching Lord Edward. When he came to claim Lady Cordelia for his waltz, she found herself unaccountably breathless as he took her hand and led her to the floor. Quite a few of the ladies in the room watched him with admiration for his handsome person, and for his skill and effortless command of the dance. Cordelia was swept up in the sensations as the room swirled around them, a kaleidoscope of colour and motion.

She was intensely aware of his hand on her waist, of the warmth of his body, so close to hers, of the subtle fragrance of leather and pine that surrounded him, mixed with something indefinable, yet somehow exciting, and of the appreciative look in his eyes as he smiled at her. Somehow, he made dancing easy – she need not concentrate on what her feet were doing at all, he simply moved and she magically moved with him. It was a sensation like none she had felt before.

After some time, the music faded to a stop, leaving Cordelia a little breathless, and oddly bereft, as the Duke courteously released his grip upon her, and escorted her back towards miss Millpost where she stood to one side. As she allowed him to lead her across the floor she saw Lord Edward, standing with his friends near the doors to the terrace.

Cordelia noticed that Lord Edward, for the first time that she could remember, was not smiling, a sullen expression on his face that she had not seen before. Perhaps he was jealous. Now that would be a truly fine thing, she thought, as the Duke led her across the floor, for, after all, the Duke was a very fine-looking gentleman indeed. Then Lord Edward's eyes met hers, and his face changed, the familiar smile greeting her warmly. Perhaps she had been mistaken before...

<div align="center">~~~~~</div>

The Duke had also caught the expression on Lord Edward's face and read a quite different message in the young man's eyes. He suspected, as he escorted the young girl from the floor, that young Fitzhugh was piqued by the fact that he was no longer the centre of attention in the room, that people's eyes had followed lady Cordelia as she danced with the Duke, instead.

That particular character trait did not bode well for Lady Cordelia Branley's future, should she become attached to the young man. It did not bode well at all.

He found, of a sudden, that he cared quite a lot about Lady Cordelia Branley's future, more than simply for the sake of his long friendship with her father. Despite his best intentions, they had barely spoken a word to each other as they danced. He had become utterly caught up in the sensation, enchanted by her unspoiled innocence of manner, and the graceful way in which she gave herself to the dance, flowing easily with him on the crowded floor. Her wide violet eyes had looked into his with delight, as if she too found the sensation wonderful. The thought crept in unexpectedly – he had not felt that way when dancing with a woman since Angelique, since that terrible night when he lost her, and their child.

Her face came to his mind at the thought, but it was no longer sharp in his memory and, astoundingly, the terrible ache in his heart, whilst still present, was muted, softened. He was not sure what to make of that – it felt a little disloyal to no longer hurt so much.

He turned his attention back to Lady Cordelia, whose prettily flushed cheeks and sparkling eyes told the tale of how much she was enjoying herself. He hoped, selfishly, that a little, at least, of the enjoyment was due to his attention to her, to that wonderful dance.

Could he dare to think that he might have truly distracted her from young Fitzhugh, even if only for a short time?

<div align="center">~~~~~</div>

Whilst the dancing filled the room with energetic movement, Baron Setford was drawn aside by a footman.

"My Lord, a messenger has just delivered this for you."

He proffered a letter on a silver salver. Setford took it, nodding his thanks. He moved to a quiet alcove, sheltered by some potted palms, and settled into a chair before breaking the seal. This was the report that he had been waiting for. His informant was a man with access to the private financial dealings of the Earl of Bolton's family. He had asked the man to report on just one aspect of the family dealings. The result was not unexpected, and could, perhaps, explain a great deal. In three sentences, his informant laid out the salient facts.

The Earl of Bolton, disgusted at his younger son's failure to follow him to war, had, more than 6 months ago, cut off all allowances to the boy, pending such time as he should take up a commission and do his patriotic duty. His brother George had honoured their father's decision – he had not responded to Lord Edward's pleas for funds, and had refused to speak to him since shortly after their father's decision. Young Lord Edward was without funds, unless he could raise them himself – which he appeared to have been doing rather successfully, at the card tables.

Setford tucked the letter into his pocket, and went in search of Rotherhithe and Tillingford. Seeing Tillingford surrounded by his guests, he turned to Rotherhithe who stood near Miss Millpost, both of them watching Lady Cordelia dance with Lord Edward, for their one allowable dance of the evening. Rotherhithe's face showed a careful casual unconcern, but his eyes followed the young couple, and there was a tightness to his posture. Interesting indeed.

"Rotherhithe, I word if I might." Setford bowed to Miss Millpost, and, at the Duke's nod of assent, led him out onto the terrace.

"I've just received a most interesting missive. Thought you should see it before the evening goes much further."

Setford passed the folded letter to Rotherhithe and waited as he perused it. After a moment's consideration of the content, the Duke passed it back to Setford.

"Well, that puts a rather different colouration on things, doesn't it? I've a suspicion I know what the young popinjay's playing at, and I don't like it, not at all. For a man in his position, Lady Cordelia's dowry would be a tempting opportunity – even more tempting than the chance to continue his 'run of luck' at the cards, wouldn't you say?"

"Exactly, Rotherhithe. I've my suspicions about that 'luck' too, but we'd need to prove it. I'd prefer that the boy's own actions expose his less than honourable intentions, if that is what they are, well before Lady Cordelia makes a commitment she may regret."

"Indeed, I couldn't agree more. I would go a long way to protect the Lady's interests. It seems, then, that I feel a strange inclination for some time at the card tables this evening."

The Duke's wry smile as he spoke brought an answering smile to Setford's face, and his deep laughter followed the Duke as he stepped back into the ballroom.

~~~~~
~~~~~

As the musicians began to tire from their exertions - and from the effects of the wine that they had consumed so enthusiastically during the evening - the guests began to move in small groups to the spacious drawing room with its comfortable seating, crystal decanters of fine cognac and a scattering of card tables.

The Ladies were fanning themselves, sipping cordials for refreshment and some of the gentlemen had already taken their seats to play a hand of cards. It was entirely permissible to wager on the outcome of each game and it was widely considered as good sport and an entertaining way to pass an evening.

Cigars were available and footmen trimmed the fine cheroots and offered tapers to light them as the players settled down to their game.

Within a half hour, a small crowd had gathered around the table where Fitzhugh was playing, and his luck was drawing gasps of amazement as he won a series of hands and gathered before him an impressive pile of gold coins.

"Pon my soul, young man, but you have the luck of the Devil himself."

A well-dressed nobleman threw down his cards and exclaimed to the onlookers.

"Five hands in a row and he has taken the prize each time! I have never seen the like. Tis sorcery and black magic! We should summon a bishop to bless the deck."

Edward smiled and raised his hands in innocence.

"Pray, good Sir, it is surely not the work of the Devil but the generous hand of Lady Fortune that favours the draw of the cards. I cannot help the way the cards fall and I do not complain that they seem to work to my advantage. Perhaps it is nothing more than beginner's luck."

His fine words soothed the gentleman's displeasure and the crowd murmured in approval at the young noble's display of tact and modesty.

Just then, the Duke stepped forward and asked if he might take the departing gentleman's place at the table. The crowd seemed excited at the prospect of watching the great man play a hand of cards. Edward looked up and bowed his head with the utmost courtesy and expressed his delight that the Duke had chosen to honour the game with his presence. Rotherhithe took his seat and placed a small, hand-tooled leather purse upon the green baize of the playing surface.

"We haven't been formally introduced. I am Philip Canterwood, Duke of Rotherhithe, and I have the honour to be acquainted with your father."

Edward smiled once again and nodded his head in respect as he shuffled the cards.

"It is an honour, Your Grace, an honour. And, as you are apparently aware, I am Lord Edward Fitzhugh, second son of the Earl of Bolton."

Lord Edward quickly dealt the cards under the watchful gaze of the Duke.

"You enjoy the gaming tables, do you not, young Fitzhugh?"

"I have played occasionally, Your Grace."

"Come, sir. You seem most uncommonly familiar with the cards, for I have rarely seen them shuffled and dealt so expertly."

"I may have a minor talent in that direction, Your Grace."

"Is that how you spend your time? Playing cards and wagering on the outcome?"

"As I said, Your Grace, I do play on occasion. But it is for pleasure rather than for the sport or for the winnings."

Lord Edward looked up from his cards at that moment and found himself staring into the Duke's steely eyes, their golden tones darkened to almost black.

"Judging by the coin you have accumulated this evening, it would seem to be a most profitable pastime for you."

"Fortune has certainly favoured me this evening, Your Grace. There is no denying it."

The gentlemen placed their wagers and, with a flourish, Lord Edward grinned and revealed his winning hand.

"I seem to be Fortune's favoured player this evening. If this continues, no one will wish to try their luck. I shall be forced to play alone!"

The crowd laughed at the young Lord's heartfelt sigh and weary complaint, yet the Duke had watched him most carefully and was strangely keen to suggest another hand.

"I am also fond of the gaming table and would wish to try my luck again. Perhaps for the sake of good sport, you would be willing to increase the wager?"

Lord Edward looked across the table and glanced down at the Duke's finely-crafted leather purse.

"But of course, Your Grace. What would you suggest?"

"Your winnings. Let that be the wager on the next turn of the cards."

Fitzhugh smiled and nodded graciously. "As Your Grace wishes."

The Duke waved his hand at the other players.

"But let us not dilute the sport with these other players, who are, I believe, your friends?"

A brief flicker crossed Fitzhugh's face before he quickly recovered his composure.

"Well, Your Grace, that would certainly make the game more interesting. Higher stakes and only two players. Very well."

The other two players stood up, glancing at each other and moving away from the table, settling to watch from the side.

Lord Edward began to shuffle the deck.

"I believe it is my turn to deal, Fitzhugh."

The Duke smiled as he extended his open hand across the table. Now there was a flush of colour around Lord Edward's finely stitched and embroidered shirt collar. He hesitated and the Duke remained with his arm outstretched, smiling and unblinking.

Cordelia had joined Miss Millpost in the circle of onlookers and could not quite understand what was going on at the table.

Lord Edward seemed more ill at ease than she had ever seen him, and the Duke, by comparison, seemed completely relaxed.

"What's happening?" she whispered to her companion.

"More than meets the eye," the older lady replied.

The Duke accepted the pack of cards and began to shuffle them, slowly, carefully, methodically, never moving his gaze from the young man seated opposite him.

"Fitzhugh." The Duke began to deal with a calm, deliberate placement of each card. "Why are you not serving with your father, the Earl, in Spain?"

The question took Lord Edward by surprise.

"Speak up. Why are you not serving with your father against the French?" The Duke's voice had taken on a hard edge, but his calm handling of the cards never slowed.

"I am waiting to be summoned to the colours in due course, Your Grace."

"Nonsense, sir. No summoning is required and well you know it. The purchase of a commission can be achieved speedily, and with no impediment for one such as you. Your place is alongside your brave and noble father who fights for King and country. Why are you not with him?"

The Duke placed the last card face down on the table and leaned forwards.

"I am waiting for your answer, Sir. Why are you not in Spain with your father, the Earl?"

"I did not come here to be harried and questioned, Your Grace."

"You will answer my question, sir, or I will demand satisfaction with my sword. For I find myself offended by your unpatriotic attitude."

The crowd of onlookers gasped and Cordelia put both hands to her mouth. She found herself torn – the Duke looked so powerful, so impressive, and she liked him, she did not wish to see these men fight. Lord Edward was all that she had thought of for months – she could not bear to see him harmed – and she felt quite certain that the Duke was more than capable of harming him in a duel.

"No," she whispered, "not a duel. Not with my sweet Edward. That cannot be allowed."

Lord Edward looked angry. "What will you have of me, Your Grace? I thought we had agreed to play a simple hand of cards and now you accuse me in front of these guests as if I were a common criminal. It is not right that you treat me so, Your Grace. It is not right!"

For the first time, his charming composure shattered - his voice rose and he was trembling.

"I have not, as yet, accused you of anything that would make you a common criminal – although, perhaps, that too could happen."

The Duke shrugged and flipped over his cards to reveal an unbeatable hand.

"It appears that you have lost the game, young Fitzhugh, and I will have your coin and I will have the truth from you. One way or another."

"Damn you, but I will show you who are trifling with!"

Lord Edward, eyes wild and an expression of desperation on his face, sprang from his seat and drew a narrow, wicked blade from his sleeve, knocking over the chair and preparing to lunge across the table at the Duke.

In that instant, a swinging blow to the back of his oiled and coiffured head, with a crystal decanter of Madeira, stunned the young aristocrat and sent him sprawling to the floor. Miss Millpost studied the glassware and declared that, happily indeed, it had not broken and, more importantly, not a single drop of the precious liquor had been spilt.

"Miss Millpost!" Cordelia wailed. "How could you? You struck Lord Edward. You could have killed him!"

"And what a tragic loss of a vain and strutting popinjay that would have made!" She turned to Cordelia and looked her squarely in the eye as she continued.

"He drew a blade and was intent upon mischief. He was fortunate that I am not a man, for if I were, the blow would surely have done far more than lay the oaf out senseless."

"Madame, that was as fine and timely a blow as I have ever been privileged to observe." The Duke bowed graciously towards Miss Millpost. "I am indebted to you for hastening to my aid. Have you considered enlisting in a regiment of Amazons and scaring the French half to death with your martial prowess?"

His voice was smooth, but an underlying edge of laughter accompanied his words, and his mouth twitched into an irrepressible smile. For the first time in her seventeen years, Cordelia swore that she saw Miss Millpost blush.

She almost appeared coy and coquettish in the face of the Duke's compliments.

Turning to a pair of footmen who were stationed at the door, the Duke instructed them to detain young Fitzhugh in the cellar. And then he added that the Lord's companions should be restrained too, on suspicion of less than honest dealings with the cards.

"By heaven but I will get to the bottom of this and learn the truth before morning."

As the swirl of agitated gossip and speculation rolled through the room, the Duke calmly offered his arm to Lady Cordelia, and escorted her from the room.

∾∾∾∾∾

Six large footmen escorted the dazed Lord Edward and his friends to the cellars, to await the decisions which would determine his future.

Baron Setford went to find Tillingford, and, after he had shown Tillingford the letter from his informant, they descended to the cellars, to await Rotherhithe before questioning the miscreants.

Chapter Ten

As the Duke escorted her from the drawing room, through the crowd of shocked, whispering, gossiping onlookers, Cordelia was in a state of total confusion. How could it be true? How could her sweet Edward have transformed so, before her eyes, into a hateful, knife wielding madman?

That moment had terrified her – the look in his eyes, his obvious intent to kill, or at least seriously harm, the Duke, was like nothing she had experienced before, except perhaps the day when, as a child, she had seen a rabid dog attack one of their grooms. She could never allow a man who could look, and behave like that to touch her. The very thought made her shiver in revulsion.

She clung to the Duke's arm, his calm strength anchoring her as the storm of her emotions raged through her. Such a contrast, she realised vaguely – the Duke's calm composure and Lord Edward's mad behaviour. Stepping out of the room, her racing heart eased, and she was grateful to sink into a chair when they reached the library. The Duke closed the door behind them, and, once she was settled, fetched her a glass of brandy.

"You've had quite a shock my dear Lady, here, sip this slowly, and let it restore your sensibilities. Shall I fetch Miss Millpost? "

The first sip of brandy sent warmth swirling back into Cordelia's body, and brought the world back into focus a little.

She realised that she was staring at the Duke, blankly, like an idiot. She took another sip.

"Miss Millpost? Perhaps... I am overset, I don't know what to think."

As the Duke turned towards the door, intent on finding Miss Millpost, it opened, and not only Miss Millpost, but Georgiana, and Mary, their maid, rushed in.

Georgiana took one look at her and rushed to her, wrapping her arms around her sister. Miss Millpost dextrously captured the glass of brandy as Georgiana's heedless hug caused it to slip from Cordelia's fingers.

"Delia, what happened? You look so white and scared!"

Georgiana's question finally freed Cordelia from her half-frozen confusion, and a tear slid down her cheek. She hugged Georgiana tight to her.

"Oh Georgie, it was so terrible! Lord Edward turned out to be not nice at all! He seemed, in fact, quite mad! When the Duke asked him some questions he reacted like a bedlamite. He went so far as to draw a knife upon the Duke!"

Georgiana gasped, turning to look at the Duke, as if seeking evidence of knife holes in his person.

The Duke spoke gently, laughter in his voice.

"No, Lady Georgiana, he did not succeed in attacking me. My person remains quite whole. With, I must say, much thanks to Miss Millpost here, who efficiently knocked the young man unconscious with a fortuitously handy decanter of madeira, before he could actually reach me with the knife."

Miss Millpost actually blushed, before Georgiana and Cordelia's startled eyes. That was twice now – truly remarkable. Georgiana turned back to Cordelia, and, in the way of all siblings, could not resist stating her opinion.

"See, I knew he wasn't worth all that fuss! I never did understand why you all thought he was so delightful, prancing about spouting poetry and waving that lace kerchief." She shuddered in an over dramatised manner as she spoke. Cordelia sniffed, and her face crumpled a little. Georgiana was instantly contrite.

"Oh, Delia, I'm so sorry – you thought you loved him, didn't you? It must hurt so much to know that he was a bad man after all."

Cordelia nodded, hugging Georgiana again.

"Yes, Georgie, I thought I loved him. That is exactly the truth of it. I must have been blind to what he was truly like, taken in by all that flattery and poetry and the like. I feel like such a fool now. I don't want it to be true that he is not at all a good man, but I cannot deny what I saw with my own eyes."

The Duke watched quietly.

"About time you came to your senses, my Lady! I never liked the young fop. Always thought he was just too good to be true."

Miss Millpost spoke with her usual firmness, and what was, unmistakably, a hint of self-satisfaction.

"Indeed, Miss Millpost, you were correct. And more correct than you knew. For, in addition to his unseemly attack on me, and his cowardly refusal to obey his father and take up arms for his country, it would seem that the young man has been cheating at cards, with the collusion of his friends, gulling half of the *ton* out of rather large sums of money for many months now. The cards he used tonight were marked."

Cordelia covered her face with her hands at this last revelation. Now she felt more the fool than ever. She had watched, and enjoyed watching, a man conduct utterly dishonest play, and steal from others. She felt deeply ashamed at the thought.

It was so obvious now that Lord Edward had intentionally taken her in, from the start, gulling her as surely as he had been gulling those he played cards with. And for what purpose? There was but one she could think of – her dowry. It was so lowering to realise that he had not cared for her, as a person, at all, only for her money. The tears ran down her face, and Georgiana patted her hand, looking rather lost for what to do. Miss Millpost, pragmatic as ever, pushed the glass of brandy back into Cordelia's hand.

"Drink that, my girl, you need it."

She took it, and sipped obediently, her eyes meeting the Duke's golden brown ones, so like the colour of the brandy, over the rim of the glass. She was, again, struck by his powerful, calm demeanour.

He was undeniably handsome, and everything about him was elegant, understated by comparison to most of the men she had met in London, yet somehow more. He made her, she realised, feel safe. That was a startling thought, for, in reality, she had rarely, if ever, before tonight's incident, felt in danger, in her life. He smiled, and unbidden, her lips curved in response and her cheeks heated as she remembered the feel of his arm beneath her hand as he had escorted her from the room.

"I must leave you with your sister and Miss Millpost now, Lady Cordelia, and seek out your father. Young Fitzhugh's fate must be decided. For we would see him punished for his transgressions, but not at the expense of his family's honour. I wish you good rest, and I look forward to your company upon the morrow." The Duke bowed over her hand, and left the room.

For some minutes, she simply sat, sipping the brandy, trying to truly take in all that had happened. Her grand Ball had certainly not turned out the way that she had expected! Oddly, the moments of the evening that stood out in her mind as wonderful, were all of those spent with the Duke of Rotherhithe. Even before Lord Edward's shocking revelation of his true character, there had been no moment of true pleasure in his company, not since the kiss by the fireplace – a memory that now made her shudder – at her own childish foolishness, to be so taken in.

When she considered it all now, there was only one conclusion she could come to. Lord Edward was like a wayward boy, stubborn and selfish, caring for no one else. The Duke, however, was, she now understood, truly an honourable man, worthy of respect in all ways. Miss Millpost's voice broke into her thoughts.

"Come Cordelia, let's get you to your bed. You need to rest, if you are to look your best tomorrow. And you, Miss Georgiana, should have been abed hours ago. Mary – do take Miss Georgiana to her bed, and I'll help Cordelia."

Cordelia, a little unsteady after the substantial glass of brandy, was only too ready to comply. As they ascended the stairs, Miss Millpost had one more thing to say.

"And Cordelia, you must, absolutely, remember to thank the Duke tomorrow, for his assistance in all ways this evening. I think he will forgive you for most scandalously forgetting to do so just now, given your harrowing experience, but you must make sure to remedy your error in the morn."

Cordelia simply nodded, allowed herself to be put to bed, and surprised herself by almost immediately falling asleep. To dream of brandy coloured eyes and being held in strong arms as she danced an endless waltz.

~~~~~

Whilst Cordelia fell into restorative sleep, the Duke joined Setford and Tillingford in the cellars, where Lord Edward and his young friends were being held under guard of six burly footmen. After a short discussion, it was agreed that Tillingford would return abovestairs and see to his guests, attempting to quiet the turmoil that the events in the card room had caused, and minimise the spread of gossip, whilst Setford and Rotherhithe questioned the young men.

The truth was far easier to discern than the Duke had expected.
~~~~~

Fitzhugh's companions, afraid for their own reputations and allowances from their families, had readily admitted to their complicity in Fitzhugh's schemes, which they had, to begin with, seen as just a bit of a lark.

As Setford's informant had reported, the Earl had been outraged by his son's reluctance to follow him into battle. The shame had cast a stain upon the Earl's honour and, rather than publicly acknowledge the disgrace, he had simply cut the young Lord off without a penny until he found his courage and joined the colours.

In order to maintain his lifestyle, Fitzhugh had conspired with his companions to regulate the card games he played, with false dealing and a marked deck. The result was that he always appeared to be uncannily lucky when, in reality, he was cheating.

Rotherhithe had, with the warning provided by the letter from Setford's informant, suspected as much, and easily, once looking for them, discovered the markings on the cards - thus allowing him to win, once he had taken control of dealing.

The Duke and Baron Setford felt honour bound to inform Fitzhugh's father and brother, but elected to keep the affair private. Gossip might spread through the *ton*, but with no actual charges laid, the nobility would, as usual, close ranks to protect their own.

The boy would be shunned in society, but his family would be well regarded for dealing with him. And deal with him they must, and fast. Rotherhithe had some ideas on how to manage that.

At the very least, he had spared Tillingford's lovely daughter the disgrace of marrying a cad and a coward. She was an enchantingly lovely girl and deserved far better than the sly and manipulative Fitzhugh.

The foolish young friends were released, after swearing an oath to discuss nothing of what had occurred, at the risk of having their father's informed of their transgressions, should they fail to stand by that oath. Young Lord Edward was a more difficult case. Even while still somewhat dazed from Miss Millpost's well placed blow, he was aggressive, arrogant and defiant, the reality of his selfish personality surfacing from under the polished surface he had previously displayed.

Eventually, though, the reality of his situation was impressed upon him. He could be charged, and sent to Newgate, with a fair chance that he would hang, or he could take up a commission that would be arranged for him, and follow his father to war. It was the choice between almost certain death, and less likely death. Should he survive the army, he could return home, with honour, and no-one the wiser about his foolish choices.

Being disinclined to die, he was wise enough to accept the course of action which his father had wanted all along. It had a dark and suitable irony to it. He was to be held in the cellars overnight, in case he took into his head any silly ideas of avoidance, and then on the morrow, Baron Setford would escort him, under guard, to his brother, arrange the commission, and see him onto a military ship. As Setford said – he might be lucky – the war seemed to be turning somewhat in their favour – perhaps he would not need to survive over there too long.

Chapter Eleven

The Baron and his friends sat in the library the next day and sipped a restorative glass of Madeira together before Setford set off once more for London.

The Baron sighed. "I will always be grateful to you, Canterwood, and you, Setford, for what you have done for Cordelia. I'm sure she will quickly get over the Fitzhugh boy."

"You are truly blessed with a fine and beautiful daughter in Cordelia, Tillingford. If I were a younger man, I'd be courting her myself."

The Baron looked at his friend.

"You are not so old, my dear Canterwood."

The men sipped their Madeira in silence for a long moment.

There was a polite knock at the door and Cordelia stepped shyly into the library and asked her father if she might intrude. The Duke smiled as he stood to greet his friend's daughter.

"Lady Cordelia. How are you feeling on this fine morning?"

She looked down at her feet, slightly overawed, in the light of a new day, by the Duke's imposing presence.

"Your Grace, I wanted to thank you for your kindness. I know that I have been a little foolish over Lord Fitzhugh's intentions, and my companion has reminded me that I owe you my gratitude for everything that you did last night. I must apologise for being in no state to than you properly at the time."

The Duke stepped forward and took Cordelia's delicate hand in his own, raising her fingertips to his lips and kissing them in a gesture of courteous respect.

"Your happiness and welfare will always be my concern, my Lady."

Cordelia raised her eyes to look into the Duke's kind face and, in that moment, her heart fluttered and she felt a warmth in her chest that quite surprised her and took her breath away. It had never occurred to her young heart that she might find a man of the Duke's maturity so attractive but his distinguished appearance and his aura of power suddenly seemed deeply alluring.

There was a twinkle in the Duke's eye that her father noticed with a wry smile. A marriage to the Duke would certainly secure Cordelia's future and, as the wife of a Duke with vast wealth and extensive lands in England and the Colonies she would be guaranteed a life of comfort and a position of influence in society.

He could see the flush in her cheeks and nodded quietly. A match made in heaven.

"My dear Canterwood," said the Baron as he raised himself with some difficulty from his comfortable chair. "I have a feeling that we might be seeing much more of you in the future and I am sure that I am not the only one who will be pleased to welcome you in this house!"

The Duke laughed, still looking at Cordelia, and he nodded his agreement.

"Aye, Tillingford. I do declare that you may well be right. You will, at least be seeing quite a bit of me for the next week or so, before I find it necessary to return to London. After that, we shall see..."

Cordelia curtsied to the Duke, who was obviously charmed and delighted by her presence, and then asked her father if she might be excused to attend to Miss Millpost who was waiting for her, as they intended to take advantage of the delightful weather, with a drive through the town and surrounding countryside. Bath, at this time of year, was a most pleasant place to be.

She left with a spring in her step and a smile on her lips, sensing that something wonderful had just taken place. At the back of her mind, she could not help trying on a new title for herself – Duchess of Rotherhithe. As she met her companion, she felt sure that the title was absolutely perfect for her. It was probably a foolish girl's thought, she admitted, yet... the Duke was, undeniably attractive, now that she truly looked at him. Her heart beat faster at the thought.

The Duke and the Baron resumed their seats and picked up their unfinished glasses of Madeira.

An unspoken agreement was unfolding between them, an understanding that involved the Duke and the young Lady Cordelia. It was as if, in a matter of moments, a new chapter had begun in their lives and it made the Duke feel younger and more vital than he had felt in many a year. He smiled as he contemplated the implications of having such a young and beautiful wife. The girl had, somehow, in just a matter of days, somehow broken through the shell he had held around him since Angelique's death, and stirred his heart. He could, he suspected, come to love her, easily. All he need do now was to engage her affections. For he would not wish a wife who did not wish to be with him.

The Baron coughed to stir the Duke from his reverie.

"But tell me, did you not take a terrible risk when you played Fitzhugh for his winnings? Heavens, Canterwood, but you might've lost."

The Duke smiled. "Might've lost, you say, Tillingford?" He laughed out loud and nearly spilled his drink. "Spotted a damnable cad and a cheat as soon as I saw him shuffle the pack - it was marked - so I shuffled the pack instead."

The Baron looked at him, uncomprehending.

"Dash it all, Tillingford. Only a fool would try to cheat a man who knows how to cheat."

The two men laughed and laughed until the tears of mirth rolled down the Baron's cheeks.

"By heavens, Rotherhithe," the Baron was still laughing. "What a pack of fools these young men are!"

Chapter Twelve

The following day, many of the house guests had left, and the small contingent who remained had decided upon a trip to the baths, to take the waters, and test whether they felt that the reputed health benefits were real. Some, who had been before, declared their faith in the efficacy, whilst others declared the opposite. Baron Tillingford took the opportunity to join them, and start doing as his physician had suggested.

Georgiana had gone with them, determined to see it first hand, no matter whether it was efficacious of not. Miss Millpost turned up her nose at the idea of sulphurous smelling waters, and declined to join them. Cordelia agreed with her, and decided on a quiet day at home, after all of the excitement of the events at the Ball.

Rotherhithe, it appeared, shared their opinion. As Cordelia sat at the pianoforte in the drawing room, playing gently for her own entertainment, he appeared in the doorway, drawn by the sweet music.

He stood for a while, watching silently, appreciating the elegant line of her neck, where the artful drape of curls fell to one side as she concentrated on playing. She was, quite obviously, lost in the music, and beautiful in her intensity.

When she at last paused between pieces, he stepped into the room, applauding. Cordelia spun on the seat, a blush rising immediately to her cheeks.

"Oh, Your Grace, I did not know you were here. I do hope that my playing has not disturbed your morning."

"To the contrary dear Lady, it has, rather, improved my morning immeasurably. Your playing is so skilled that I could almost see the birds and flowers in a summer field, the music invoked such a sense of peace. I am sorry to have disturbed _you_. But… I was seeking you, to ask if you would care to join me for a walk in the gardens, to enjoy the quiet on this fine summer morning?"

Cordelia rose, a smile lighting her face, and she looked to where Miss Millpost sat, on the other side of the room, embroidering what seemed to be a cushion cover. Miss Millpost looked up, a wide smile on her face.

"Oh, you two go and enjoy yourselves, I'll just keep an eye on you through the terrace doors here. I want to finish this embroidery today!"

Cordelia blinked in surprise, a little stunned, for Miss Millpost was generally an absolute stickler for propriety. Then she shook herself out of her amazement and took full advantage of the opportunity presented to her.

"Why certainly, Your Grace, I would be delighted."

He offered her his arm, and she stepped forward to take it, intensely aware of everything about him, finding herself a little breathless and suddenly warm. That sense of safety surrounded her, and she knew, suddenly, that he cared for her, this deeply honourable, quiet, powerful man. His simple sincerity, his plain speaking, which had once seemed dull and austere, she now understood to be more valuable than any flattery, for they showed his true feelings, undisguised. That was worth more to her than any pretty flattery, covering a hollow shell.

~~~~~

He watched her face as they walked, pleased with what he saw there. Each time he was in her presence, she enchanted him further, and it seemed, from her expression, that she was not averse to his company either. They strolled through the gardens, the scent of the early summer flowers surrounding them, the only sounds the faint sounds of the horses in the stables and the buzz of the bees around the flowers. He had not felt so peaceful in years. Such a simple thing, to make him so happy.

But he needed to be sure of her feelings, her thoughts, for it would not do at all, if she still harboured some tenderness for that young fool Fitzhugh.

"Lady Cordelia, I am glad to see you looking so well today. I had feared that the events of the last few days might have left you distressed and unwell. I know that you were fond of Lord Edward, and it must be most unpleasant to know that he has disappointed you in this terrible way."
~~~~~

She stopped, and he, perforce, stopped as well. She turned to him, taking a deep breath and meeting his eyes fully. Her eyes were windows to her soul, full of sincerity and sadness. He fell into them, suddenly lost to all else.

"You are correct. In truth, I fancied myself in love with the man, I was so taken in by all of his pretty ways. I was a foolish child, looking for a fairytale, and so taken in by the pretty packaging that I could not see the man underneath. Of a certainty, I am deeply disappointed by his behaviour. But I am even more disappointed in myself. I had, before, always thought myself a good judge of character, and a sensible person." She blew out a little huff of air, which expressed her frustration completely. "It seems that my sister is correct after all, and I am a woolgathering ninnyhammer who can't see what is clearly before her face."

He laughed, a joyful appreciation of her courage, her truthfulness, and her self-deprecating humour, then lifted her hand to his lips, watching her face as turned it over and placed a kiss, with slow intensity, on her palm, his lips resting there for far longer than propriety deemed suitable. She flushed again, her eyes sparkling with something that looked like excitement and perhaps, he dared hope, the beginnings of desire.

"My dear Lady, I must greatly admire your honesty, and your courage in seeing the unpleasant truth. But that is in the past now. The young man will, undoubtedly, learn from his mistakes. As, it seems, you already have from yours. I fear that I am not one for flowery phrases, or light banter, so, perhaps my words will not thrill you as his did, but I am compelled to speak nonetheless."

He held her gaze, his warm brandy eyes shining with sincerity, and his grip on her fingers, which he had not yet released, grew tighter.

"Lady Cordelia, I find you most beautiful, and admirable in all ways. I should like to know you better. If you will permit it, I will be more than delighted to spend time with you over the coming weeks, to take you to the Assembly rooms, to drive out through the countryside, and to ride with you wherever you may wish to go. Will you do me the honour of allowing me to engage you in these activities?"

His heart pounded in his chest as he awaited her answer, and he felt more alive than he had in many years. He was terrified that she would refuse him this.

She simply stood, as if absorbing his words, a look of almost disbelief on her face. She nibbled on her lower lip as she considered, and his body tightened in response.

"I... I am most honoured, Your Grace, I would enjoy any of the activities that you have suggested. I find your direct manner most refreshing and... I would like to know you better, also."

Her smile was radiant, and he found himself smiling in return, as a warmth of happiness and relief washed through him. It was a beginning, an opportunity which he had no intention of wasting.

~~~~~
~~~~~

True to his word, the Duke spent his time with Cordelia almost every day of the next few weeks, extending his stay well past the time that he had originally intended to depart.

Chapter Thirteen

They drove out around the countryside, with Miss Millpost for chaperone, they rode out with a groom following discretely, stopping for delightful picnics in seclude spots, they attended the dances at the assembly rooms, where the other ladies present followed Cordelia with envious eyes as the Duke escorted her everywhere, and danced with her a little more often than was proper, and each day was more delightful than the one before.

Cordelia found herself drifting about dreamily at times, here mind full of the sound of his voice, the smell that was uniquely his, the feel of his lips on her hand when he kissed it, and every other tiny thing that made him the person that he was. The longer she knew him, the more his honesty, sincerity and plain speaking appealed to her.

Miss Millpost appeared to heartily approve, and often intentionally left them almost completely alone – which, whilst it utterly shocked Cordelia at first, was something she rapidly came to deeply appreciate.

Even Georgiana, who Cordelia had fully expected to be unimpressed, had surprised her by turning to her one morning and saying, "I like him. He actually cares about you. He's even nice to me, and Miss Millpost. Maybe you should marry the Duke."

Cordelia had giggled, hugged Georgiana, and left it at that. But secretly, she was very pleased. She would not want to marry a man that her sister hated.

One afternoon a week or two after that first walk in the gardens, they were strolling there again. They stopped in a secluded spot, where a bench, shaded by trees which screened it from the house, overlooked a small pond, and settled comfortably beside each other.

It seemed so natural now, to sit beside him like this. Cordelia sighed in delight, and the Duke slid his arm around her waist, drawing her to him, her head naturally falling to rest upon his shoulder. She tilted her head and looked up at him, their eyes connected, and seemingly in slow motion, his mouth came down to hers, his lips gentle, then stronger on her own, his tongue slipping out to trace the line of her lips, to tease and taste, as she sighed and melted into him. His tongue slid into the gap of her lips where the sigh had escaped, and she shivered at the taste of him, the feel of his tongue reaching for hers, exploring. It was better than she could have imagined – so much more than that tiny brush of lips from Lord Edward, which had once so excited her.

Minutes or hours passed, and warmth flooded through her body, heating her in ways and places she had not felt before, and she simply gave herself to te wonderful sensation, feeling safe and treasured in his arms.

Eventually, he drew back, smiling, his golden brown eyes glowing, and reached to gently tug her bonnet back into place, from where they had pushed it as they kissed.

It was a wonderful day.

The following day, however, was far more difficult.

~~~~~

In the evenings, once the ladies had retired, Rotherhithe had been spending his time with Baron Tillingford, finding as much joy in appreciating his old friend's company while the man still lived, as he was finding in lady Cordelia's company during the day.

But, whilst the company was wonderful, the conversation, perforce, touched on subjects that were not. The Duke had been working hard to convince Tillingford to tell the girls, and his staff, the truth about his health. Now that all of those who had come for the house party had departed, except for the Duke, the time had come to deal with that issue.

"My dear friend, I fear the time has come to tell them – you cannot put it off any longer. I swear that you grow more frail by the day. Despite your physicians hopes, those odorous waters do not seem to have worked a miracle."

"Ah, Rotherhithe, would that they had. I regretfully have to agree – it is time to tell them. It leaves me heartsick to think how they will react, yet it would be worse if I did not tell them, and they lost me without warning. I will call everyone together after luncheon tomorrow. But I will tell the girls first, in the morning. I depend upon your support at the time."
~~~~~

"Of course, I will do whatever I can to assist you."

"There is one thing you can do to assist me right now, Rotherhithe. You can tell me if you're going to marry my daughter."

The Duke laughed, amused at the Baron's somewhat belligerent tone.

"Old friend, I very much hope so. For Lady Cordelia has captured my heart, as I thought no woman ever would again, after Angelique died. I am almost certain that she has developed feelings for me – I blush to tell you that I kissed her yesterday, and she most certainly showed no objection – quite the opposite!"

"Good, good. Do ask her soon. If I don't manage to last long enough to see the wedding, I at least want to know that she'll have you!"

"So do I, more than you can imagine…"

Smiling, comfortable with their agreement, and having long ago discussed the distribution of moneys and properties that the Baron had arranged for his daughters, the old friends settled back in their chairs, for one last evening of peaceful company, before the impending tragedy began to disturb the house.

~~~~~

Cordelia tapped on the door of her father's study, a little nervously – whatever could he want? When bidden to enter, she opened the door, and Georgiana and miss Millpost followed her in, closing the door behind them.
~~~~~

Her father sat at his desk, and the Duke sat in a chair near the window. They both looked alarmingly serious.

"Yes father? You wanted to see us?"

"Do sit down, all of you, please. There is something I need to tell you." The Baron's voice was a little shaky, and his expression sad. They sat, Georgiana uncharacteristically quiet, and waited for him to go on. He looked at them all, hesitant, as if unsure what to say, where to start, then glanced at the Duke, who nodded imperceptibly. Taking a deep breath, the Baron began.

"Cordelia and Georgiana, you know that you have been the most important thing in my life. I am proud of you both – you have grown into beautiful young women. It is my fondest desire to see you both married and happy in your life. Unfortunately, it seems that I may not be able to do that."

"Why?" Georgiana, forthright as ever, did not hesitate to ask.

"Because, dear daughter, I am ill. Very ill. I have been for some time. I am sure that you have noticed that I have been coughing more taen is good, that I do things more slowly than I used, and that I have become rather thinner over the last few months. My physician tells me that it is the consumption. He had hoped that, by taking the waters here in Bath, my condition might improve – but, alas, the waters have done nothing for me. It seems likely that I will not be here to care for you much longer."

Cordelia, gave a small strangled sounding sob at his words, Georgiana simply stared at him, her face a picture of stubborn denial.

Miss Millpost paled, and watched the girls closely, unsure how to help them at this terrible moment, and rather distraught herself that her employer of so many years was dying. Cordelia stood, and paced about the room, unable to contain her distress.

"Oh Father, surely there is something that can be done! I cannot bear the thought of losing you." Her voice broke, and a tear rolled down her cheek. The Duke ached for her, but stood silent as the Baron continued.

"Alas, my dear, there is nothing. I have had to come to terms with that fact. And, having done so, I have prepared. All of the necessary papers are drawn up. There is a substantial dowry for each of you, and for each of you, some of the properties that I own, to be yours, always – there will be clauses in your marriage contracts, to prevent them becoming your husband's property. This house, Cordelia, will be yours, and Casterfield Grange, Georgiana, will be yours. There are other properties, but those are the main ones."

The girls looked at each other, Cordelia silently crying, Georgiana's face showing her dawning realisation that her father's words were true, that she would soon lose him. The Baron went on, desperate to have everything said, torn apart by watching the girls' reaction.

"Sadly, I do not know what will happen to the Barony. I have no male heir, and, within the Branley bloodline, none can be found, no matter how distant. I would therefore seem likely that I will be the last Branley to hold the noble title of Tillingford."

Georgiana, in particular, looked horrified at the concept.

"The most likely outcome is that the Prince Regent will grant the title and entailed lands to a person of his choice, once I am gone. Let us hope that he chooses wisely. Tillingford Castle will pass to the new Baron. Before I pass on, we will visit it, one last time, so that you may choose what paintings and other items from there you wish for your own. Now that I am so close to joining her in the hereafter, I will be glad to find myself amongst my memories of your mother again. After luncheon, I will speak to the staff, and inform them of all of this as well."

Georgiana burst into tears, and flung herself into Miss Millpost's arms, feeling, once again, like a small child. Miss Millpost's own tears slid down her cheeks, and fell into Georgiana's hair.

Cordelia, seeing Georgiana's reaction, finally lost control of her own sobs, and turned, covering her face with her hands. Moments later, she felt strong arms surrounding her, and the Duke pulled her against him, cradling her to his chest as she cried.

The Baron rose, tears finally escaping his own eyes, and walked slowly to where Cordelia and the Duke stood. He stroked Cordelia's hair gently, looking the Duke in the eye as he spoke.

"Cordelia, I am so glad that you have found companionship and, dare I hope, love, with my old friend Rotherhithe. I will feel better when I pass, knowing that you have him to care for you."

The Duke nodded once, and tightened his arms around Cordelia. The Baron then turned to Georgiana and Miss Millpost. He opened his arms and enfolded them both, finding himself, for a moment, unable to speak until Georgiana looked up at him.

"Georgiana, I must hope that you find a noble gentleman worthy of your keen intelligence and unique perspective on life. I am sure that Rotherhithe will be true to my wishes and do everything he can to see you well married and safe in your life. And you, Miss Millpost, I thank you, more than I can express, for all these years of service, and I beg you, stay with the girls until they are both happily married and settled, however long that may take. "

Miss Millpost nodded, finding herself, for perhaps the first time in her life, bereft of words.

"Rest assured, I have made sure, in my will, that you will be well off, and set for the rest of your life, Miss Millpost. There is an annuity, and that cottage in Casterfield Village that you have always most admired. My man of business has been instructed to ensure that you will want for nothing."

Miss Millpost simply clasped his hand and nodded.

~~~~~

When all of the staff had gathered in the ballroom, the Baron informed them of the details. There were shocked gasps, and some tears from the housekeeper and Cook, who, with Garrig, had been with him for decades.

Garrig simply drew himself up and bowed before speaking.

"Your wishes will be honoured in all things, My Lord – simply inform me of anything you need or want, and I will ensure it is done."
~~~~~

"My thanks, to all of you, for your dedication. We will remain in residence here until late August, and I will continue to take the waters, in the faint hope that they may prolong my life, and then we will remove to Tillingford Castle for a few weeks, before returning to Casterfield Grange. Please arrange things in advance according to that schedule."

Garrig bowed again, and ushered the staff from the room, leaving the Baron standing, alone, and staring, unseeing, out across the terrace and gardens.

~~~~~

A week later, once the shock of the Baron's announcement had worn off a little, and all had come to terms with the situation, The Duke excused himself from their company, to travel to his estates, and to London, to ensure that all of his personal affairs were in order, suitable for an extended absence.

He promised to return as soon as possible, and to stay with them until his old friend's end.

Cordelia, whilst missing him terribly whilst he was away, was overwhelmingly grateful that he was able to grant them so much of his time. A few weeks wait to see him again, even though it seemed interminable, was small price to pay for his presence in the coming months.

~~~~~

The Duke missed Cordelia fully as much as she missed him. The necessary absence brought home to him the fact that he did not, in future want to spend too long apart from her ever again.

He wanted to be fully sure of her affections before he asked her to marry him, and, quite obviously, he was not going to push things in this next few months, when her emotional state would be understandably fragile – but he wished, now, that he could hurry things.

He was amused at himself – all of these years since Angelique's death, he had avoided marriage minded women, and now he was the impatient one!

Chapter Fourteen

The following few months were full of bittersweet joy, as they all consciously appreciated every day that the Baron remained alive.

That joy was added to in late June, when the news of the great victory at Waterloo reached them. It seemed beyond belief that, after 20 years of war, it should be over, yet all reports suggested that was fact – that as soon as the treaty could be signed in Paris, all of England's soldiers would be coming home for good.

Cordelia, upon hearing the news, was glad for another reason – this meant that Lord Edward would now, almost certainly, be able to return home and start life afresh. Not that she wished to see him – that would be far too embarrassing after her so foolish infatuation, but she wished him well – he had never deserved to die, for his boyish bad choices.

Weeks drifted into months, and as the summer waned, so did Baron Tillingford's health, and it was obvious that he would not live a great deal longer.

The Duke, by now deeply and irrevocably certain that he wanted Cordelia as his wife, resolved to wait no longer to ask her. No matter the difficulties they faced, he wished to see the Baron's face when he could confirm their betrothal.

One late August day, as the servants were packing the house for their remove to Tillingford Castle, the Duke and Cordelia walked in the gardens, coming to rest again on the sheltered bench where he had first kissed her. With the golden light of summer's end casting her beautiful face in soft relief, she took his breath away.

"Cordelia, my darling, I know that your father's fading health wears on you terribly, and this is, perhaps not the best time for what I am about to say, yet I have come to love you with such a passion that I find myself unable to wait any longer. I must ask you. Lady Cordelia Branley – will you do me the honour of becoming my wife?"

As she had that first day, when he had asked to see more of her, to get to know her, she stared at him a moment, worrying her lower lip between her teeth. As then, the sight of it tightened his body and brought heat to every part of him. As then, he hung in torment, waiting for her answer. And then her face was transformed by a smile which lit her eyes and allowed his heart to continue beating.

"Philip...." her voice was a warm whisper of sound, his name wonderful upon her lips, "yes, oh yes, I would like that more than anything, for I have come to love you too."

His arms surrounded her, and he kissed her, the kiss an echo of that first kiss, but deeper, more passionate, expressing everything he felt for her, and could not put into words.

An hour later, they stood before Baron Tillingford, where he rested in the deep wingback chair in the study, their fingers entwined, their faces glowing with the joy of their love declared, and told him of their commitment to each other. The Baron's eyes filled with tears as his happiness overflowed. This was what he had wanted. He had begun to doubt that it would ever happen, no matter what reassurances Rotherhithe had offered – now that uncertainty was gone.

"Publish the banns. I think I can make it through another month, to have everything done properly. Once we reach Tillingford Castle, we will hold a betrothal party – a last event for the old place before it becomes someone else's problem, eh? But a word now. If I do fail in my plans, and have the inconsideration to die on you before the day, you are absolutely not to observe a full year of mourning. Six months will be more than enough. I'll put it in my will, and the gossips of the *ton* be damned if they disapprove. I'll not hold you from each other as a result of my bad timing, for any longer than absolutely necessary. Promise me that you'll do what I wish."

"Of course..." Cordelia and the Duke spoke at the same time, then paused, smiling at each other.

"Thank you, father, for that order – whilst I wish you alive and with me for as long as possible, I deeply appreciate your intent."

"Good, good, now you two run off and tell everyone else. And get Garrig to summon my man of business, so we can get that direction about the mourning into my will."

For a house in which a man waited to die, it was an astoundingly happy place that day.

~~~~~

As Tillingford's health had steadily declined, the Duke had been keeping Baron Setford apprised of events. As it became completely clear, even as early as June, that Tillingford was likely to be gone by year's end, Setford made the decision to speak to the Prince Regent as soon as possible. The great victory at Waterloo provided, fortuitously, the reason to do so with all haste, and the opportunity that Setford had been looking for.

When the Prince Regent summoned him, not long after the news of the victory arrived, to discuss the changes which would be needed in Setford's work, managing the clandestine work that kept the nation's secrets, and the Prince regent himself safe, as well as discovering enemy plans before they could be actioned, Setford took the chance to raise another subject as well.

"Your Highness, I believe that you are well aware of my most effective group of field agents – the six men that the soldiers have dubbed 'His Majesty's Hounds'?"

"Indeed, spymaster, I am greatly appreciative of what they have achieved. But, Setford, knowing you, I must assume you've a reason for reminding me of their existence today. Out with it. And I hope it doesn't spoil my pleasure in the fact that this damned war seems to be finally over."

"You, as always, see right through me, Your Highness." Setford smiled a self-deprecating smile, knowing full well that what he had just said was empty flattery. But it worked. The Prince Regent waved him to continue.
~~~~~

"They have all notified me that, as soon as the last of the treaties are dealt with, they wish to reign their commissions, and return to their civilian lives. I am loathe to lose such skilled operatives completely. It seems to me that, if we wish to retain their services in any way, it would be best if they are kept able to be in close contact with each other, and, for at least some of them, feeling a sense of obligation – to you, Your Highness."

The Prince Regent's eyes narrowed, but he nodded and waited – Setford would get to the point in his own way.

"Of the six, two are not of the nobility. One is a merchant – now a rather wealthy merchant, as it happens, and I am looking at ways in which that may be of service to the crown, whilst keeping his interest engaged. That is a discussion for another time. The other is the son of some minor landed gentry. A solid man, and one who has performed some of the most unpleasant, but necessary work, if you understand my meaning. He is the subject of this conversation. For I believe that I have a solution to offer you, to both keeping him 'obliged' and to another issue – one of which you are not yet aware."

"Interesting. I see no objection to anything you've said so far. But tell me, what is this 'other issue'?"

"A man that I have known for many years, one Baron Tillingford, is about to die. He is far gone with the consumption, and unlikely to last out the year. That, in itself, is not an issue. The issue is that he has no heir. There is not even a far distant male relative of any kind. When he dies, 800 years of his family history with the Barony dies with him."

"No heirs, you say? Are you certain?"

"Quite, Your Highness.   Extensive investigation has been carried out to confirm it. He has two daughters, and adequate unentailed properties and funds to ensure their comfort and good marriages, but no heir at all. So the title and the entailed estates, will revert to the crown upon his death. He, and his ancestors, have all been excellent stewards of the land, and he is, even as his health declines, still deeply concerned about the fate of his lands and tenants. It seems to me that this presents an opportunity. Should you see your way to grant the title and estates of the Barony of Tillingford to young Gerald Otford, in recognition of his outstanding service to the crown, it would relieve you of the need to manage the estates, and bind young Otford to you, in obligation for the great honour you will have bestowed upon him. It will also mean that, as a man with a title, he will be more welcome, more able to move amongst the *ton*, in close contact with the other 'Hounds', and thus be infinitely more useful to us in the future."

The Prince Regent was silent, considering Setford's words. Setford simply sat, waiting, his piercing grey eyes taking in every nuance of the Prince Regent's expression.   Eventually, his patience was rewarded.

"I see no issue with your plan, Setford. I am quite certain that you have some underlying intent which you may have neglected to mention to me, but in light of the service you have provided, and will continue to provide, I will overlook that suspicion for now. You will have your way. Provide me all of the details, and the letters of patent and grant of arms will be drawn up, and held ready, pending the time of the current Baron's death."

Baron Setford bowed deeply, hiding his smile as he did so.

"As you command, Your Highness."

~~~~~

They spent September at Tillingford Castle, the Baron deep in memory of his time there with his wife, but glad to see the place one more time. His daughters, who had barely visited the ancient house since their mother's death, explored everything. With the help of the Duke, they chose what things they most wished to keep, mainly trinkets and paintings of their mother, plus a few pieces of furniture, and had them shipped to Casterfield Grange.

A betrothal party was arranged and celebrated quietly, in deference to the Baron's ailing state, but, quiet or not, it was a day of great joy for them all. It was over all too soon, and the time came to close up the great house and leave. That last day was deeply sombre, for all new that no Branley would ever walk these halls again as rightful Lord and owner. The shrouding of the rooms in dust cloths, and the closing of the doors seemed like an echo of the approaching winter, and the Baron's approaching death.

~~~~~

At Casterfield Grange, the warmth of their beloved home enclosed them and it seemed unlikely that the Baron would live until the first days of October, which had been set as the wedding date. He refused to give up, and forbade them from changing anything, saying it would all be as God willed. God's will, in the end, was that the Baron would not see Cordelia's wedding day.

He had received a letter from Baron Setford and, upon opening it, smiled, and released a great sigh of relief. He handed the letter to the Duke, then waved him from the room.

"Leave me sleep old boy, I've no energy for anything now."

The Duke left him and, that night, he slipped away in his sleep, one week to the day before the wedding was scheduled. What had been planned as a day of joy became, instead, the day of a funeral. An enormous number of people attended, to Cordelia and Georgiana's surprise – they had never quite realised how many people's lives their father had touched.

There were many tears, and many long conversations, both reminiscences and planning of the future, there was, a week or so later, the formal reading of the will. A will that no one was likely in any way to contest, there being no other relatives beyond the girls and Cousin Mathilde, to care about it. Both Cordelia and Georgiana were stunned at the size of the dowries settled upon them, and at the number of properties they had actually been given. Miss Millpost nearly fainted when told the size of the annuity granted her, to be paid regularly, from the time that Georgiana married.

There was only one surprise in the entire content of the thing – a clause that Georgiana rather resented, no matter how much she had loved her Papa. Simply put, it stated that the control of the properties and funds left to her would not actually pass to her until she married. Until then, The Duke of Rotherhithe would manage them in trust for her.

It was determined that Cordelia and the Duke could not, now, marry before the following May, even with the Baron's wishes about a shorter period of mourning.

Neither of them was happy about the delay, but there was little choice.

It was agreed that the girls would live at Casterfield Grange, with Miss Millpost as companion, and with an estate manager, appointed by the Duke, to help them. Georgiana promised herself that, no matter what anyone else thought proper, she would learn every tiny thing she could about the management of the estates, as soon as possible. Papa had left them to her, and it was right that she honour him by learning how best to care for the home where she had grown up.

The Duke promised to visit very frequently, as much as possible, around keeping his own estates in order. The wedding, when it finally came, was to be held at Canterwood Park, and the Duke assured the girls that they would be welcome to reside there in the last weeks before the wedding, to make all arrangements easier.

It was all rather a whirlwind of change, and Cordelia and Georgiana both felt helplessly swept along by events.

~~~~~

The chill of winter was sharp in the wind on the day when six men stepped onto the London docks, and back into civilian life for the first time in many years.

After nearly a decade of living closely with each other, saving each other's' lives, and caring only for survival, with no need to deal with polite society, they all felt somewhat unmoored from reality, as they breathed the London air.
~~~~~

They had agreed, while aboard the ship, that this first night, they would take rooms in a better quality of Inn, together, before braving separation and reunion with their families on the morrow. As they stepped away from the dock, however, a gentleman stepped down from a large, plain carriage, and walked towards them. He was of average height, with mid brown hair, and dressed in plain, but elegantly tailored clothing of the best quality. His piercing grey eyes assessed their appearance, and he smiled.

"Well met, gentlemen. I am glad to see you all returned, whole and hearty. Are you ready to take up the reins of your daily lives again?"

One of the men stepped forward, his hand outstretched, and returned the smile of greeting.

"Baron Setford! What brings you to greet us? I had thought, with us resigning our commissions, that we might well expect not to be seeing you again."

"Ah Hunter, or, as I should say now, I suppose, Your Grace, did you really think to be rid of me so easily?"

"Perhaps not, had I thought on it at all." Baron Setford laughed heartily in response to the other man's words.

"Well then, be glad I'm here, for you'll travel in comfort now. Gather your belongings, and lets away. The coach is big enough for all of us, and I've rooms already arranged for you at a cosy inn – not too upscale – you'll not be tripping over members of the *ton* until you're ready. We've a few things to discuss, before you scatter to live your ordinary lives."

∼∼∼∼∼

Two hours later, in the private parlour of a quality Inn on the fringes of the fashionable area of London, Baron Setford sat with the six, who were now washed, shaved and dressed in rather cleaner and newer clothes than any they'd had access to for years, and addressed himself to the substantial supper laid before them

Setford had not only provided the rooms, but the clothes, which he had miraculously managed to deliver in exactly the correct sizes and styles to suit, as well as the services of a valet, one Bulwick, to assist them. A valet who was truly scandalised at the state they were in, and determined to remedy it, at once.

As the day became evening, and the evening deep night, Setford told each of them what he knew of the state of their families, the events of recent times in London, in the *ton* and more, giving them the gift of re-entering society prepared to deal with it. When he came, last, to Gerald Otford, he smiled, and produced, from the pocket of the overcoat that he had laid casually aside, hours ago, a rather large envelope, sealed with a most impressive seal. Setting it on the table beside him, he proceeded to ignore it as he spoke, causing all of them to cast curious glances at it.

"Gerald, m'boy, you'll be glad to hear that your father is well, no matter what he may claim, and still as well liked as Squire in the parish as always. All of your family are well, in fact, and remarkably unremarkable in every way. I'd be inclined, at risk of offending you, to call them boring."

Gerald's face fell at Setford's words. The thought of settling back into his family, amidst the bucolic splendour of the Gloucestershire countryside, of having his father and older brother attempt to direct his life, made him shudder. He would go quite mad (well, more so than the dreams and memories of things that he had done during the war already made him). But he had no idea what else he would do.

"However…" Setford's eyes lit with an almost mischievous spark as he paused a moment, "I have here something that may save you from that fate rather nicely."

He passed the envelope to Gerald, and sat back, an almost smug look upon his face, waiting.

Gerald, knowing well that anything presented like that by Setford had an equal chance of being simply positive, or positively dangerous, looked at the envelope in his hand as if the thing might bite him. After a few minutes Charlton spoke up, in a smooth voice with an edge of laughter in it.

"For God's sake, Gerry, open the damn thing. We're all dying to know what's in it!"

Gerald allowed himself to look at it, closely, for the first time. The seal was large, and, now he looked, immediately recognisable.

"The Prince Regent?" There was disbelief in his voice, but Setford nodded.

Breaking the seal, Gerald unfolded the paper, and pulled out the other sheets enclosed. As he began to read the top one, his eyes widened in shock, and he swallowed, his breathing unsteady all of a sudden.

Quickly he read the other sheets, and then re-read each one. The tension in the room stretched thin, as the others realised that something very significant was happening in front of them. Eventually Gerald looked up at their expectant faces, and spoke.

"It would seem that, through some unknown mechanism," he glanced rather pointedly at Setford, who looked totally unruffled at the implication, "the Prince Regent has become aware of my... services rendered... for the crown during the war. He has chosen to reward me, for some reason known only to him. With a title, and estates, it seems."

After a moment, Hunter nodded, smiling and asked, "Who have you become then? How should we address you now...."

"It seems that I am now Gerald Otford, Baron Tillingford, and I am the possessor of a number of estates, including something called Tillingford Castle, in Berkshire."

The others applauded, and raised their drinks in a toast, and the evening descended into tale telling and merriment, as the reality of being home in England, and safe, began to settle into their bones.

Setford watched them closely, and saw the moment of disappointment, almost bitterness on Raphael's face. Raphael Morton was the only other Hound without a title. And, it seemed that, as Setford had suspected, even being rich as Croesus, from the mercantile empire that his late father had built, did not quite remove the bitterness of being an untitled Cit in a world of titled men.

Well, time would see about that. For now, they needed to take back their lives.

~~~~~

Before Christmas, as the others each worked to find their feet in society again, Gerald travelled to Berkshire and began the process of transforming himself from a quiet country Squire's second son into a man of power and authority in society. It wasn't easy, and he spent most of his time feeling spectacularly like a fraud. But at least it minimised the time he need spend stultifying with his family.

Some time in London, and a few evenings with the other Hounds, around the end of January, eased the transition. The others promised to help him navigate the deep waters of the *ton*, and laughed with him about the odd things found in very old country houses.

In mid-February, Setford visited him, unexpectedly, and suggested, quietly, that there were some people he should meet. Intrigued, Gerald asked why.

"I expect by now you've learned, from the staff at Tillingford Castle, how the title and lands came to be available for the Prince Regent to grant them to you. What you may not know, is that the previous Baron had two daughters, and a few friends, me amongst them, who cared a great deal about what became of his heritage. I'd like you to meet his daughters, so that they can see what sort of a man now walks in their father's shoes."

Gerald's stomach suddenly churned. From what he'd heard of the previous Baron, there was a lot to live up to – how could he possibly seem enough, in the eyes of the man's daughters? Still, how could he not agree?
~~~~~

Chapter Fifteen

Christmas passed quietly at Casterfield Grange, the joy of the season dulled by the aching emptiness of the old Baron's absence. As January became February, Georgiana immersed herself in estate management, farming strategy, financial planning and everything else required to maintain a property well.

The estate manager appointed by the Duke, at first hesitant about involving a sixteen-year-old gently reared lady in such messy matters as cattle breeding and cropping, was soon won over by her obvious intelligence and plain speaking, as well as her complete lack of such ladylike habits as fits of the vapours. Georgiana was made of sterner stuff, and he respected it.

The Duke visited often, and the love he felt for Cordelia only grew with every visit, as did hers for him. Georgiana still regarded them with some bemusement, but had begun to admit, in her heart of hearts, that perhaps being loved with such sincerity would not be a bad experience after all. If she must marry to claim her inheritance, then she would wish for a love like theirs.

The Duke had informed them, when he had visited shortly before Christmas, that the Prince Regent had, as they had expected, granted the title and lands of Tillingford to another man. A war hero, from all reports, a man who was young for the honour, but had provided such service to the crown that he was worthy of being rewarded in such a way.

The girls had been curious, but, so soon after their father's death, unable to imagine greeting another as 'Baron Tillingford'. The Duke had let the matter drop, but wondered how they would feel in a few months' time. Hence, when Baron Setford sent a message, in early February, suggesting that he bring the new Baron Tillingford to Casterfield Grange, that the girls might meet him, and be at peace with knowing how well their father's heritage was cared for, he had cautiously raised the subject again.

Cordelia had paled, and sat silent for some time. Georgiana had looked more considering, a light of irrepressible curiosity in her eyes. Eventually, Cordelia came to a decision.

"My dear Philip, I believe you are right. I think that I would like to meet this man, that the crown has found worthy of filling my father's place. It would allow me to go more easily forward into our life together if I know that my father's work is honoured, and the tenants that he cared for so well will be treated as they should be."

Georgiana nodded.

"I too would like to see him. With all that I have now learnt about the management of estates, I am greatly concerned for the welfare of the tenants of the Tillingford estates, even if they are no longer ours."

"It's settled then. I will arrange it. I believe that Baron Setford will escort him here, and introduce you."

~~~~~

So it was that, one clear frosty day in late February, with their mourning period nearly half done, and Cordelia's wedding no longer seeming so impossibly far distant, they waited nervously in the front parlour.

Cordelia, unable to help herself, was peeking out through the curtains, much to the Duke's amusement, when an elegant carriage came into view, passing between the winter bare trees that lined the driveway, revealed as if by magic as the midday sun burnt off the last of the drifting mists of morning. She dropped the curtain and turned back to the room, suddenly unsure of the wisdom of this meeting. But it was too late now.

"They are here." She was chagrined to discover that her voice shook as she spoke.

The Duke rose, and offered her his arm, indicating that Georgiana should come to his other side.

"Let us greet them in the foyer, ladies."

He led them from the room.

Moments later, the sound of carriage wheels on gravel was followed by a firm knock upon the door. Garrig opened it, on his most pompous ceremony as butler, and there was a moment of complete silence.
~~~~~

In the doorway, beside Baron Setford, stood an unassuming gentleman – well dressed, in a quiet way, handsome, with strong cheekbones and distinctive deep blue eyes, and thick dark blonde hair which was already curling a little in escape from the structured styling that his valet had obviously attempted to impress upon it.

It was instantly obvious to Cordelia that he was as nervous as she was. She couldn't blame him, she supposed, this must be just as strange for him as for them. The moment passed, the gentlemen entered the foyer, Garrig closed the door, and introductions proceeded. Baron Setford bowed.

"So lovely to see you again, Ladies. Lady Cordelia, Lady Georgiana, may I present Lord Gerald Otford, newly Baron Tillingford."

Gerald bowed over each Lady's hand, then turned, enquiringly, towards the Duke. Setford continued.

"And this is Philip Canterwood, the Duke of Rotherhithe, Lady Cordelia's betrothed."

"Delighted, Your Grace." Gerald's bow showed exactly the correct degree of deference.

The Duke smiled broadly, as they moved into the parlour.

"It will take me a while to get used to calling you Tillingford, I'm afraid. I knew the old Baron for more than twenty years, so the idea of someone else with the name is odd for me."

"That's completely understandable, Your Grace, perhaps you would find it more comfortable to call me Otford?"

"Thank you. An excellent idea!"

The tension in the room became obviously less at this exchange, and, as they all settled into chairs, Cordelia rang for refreshments. Conversation was initially rather stilted, until Gerald asked the question most dear to his heart at that point.

"Ladies, Your Grace, may I ask, if it's not too personal, that you tell me something of my predecessor, of his wishes for his lands, and any plans that he may have had for the estates, which were cut short by his most unfortunate demise?"

A look passed between the Duke and Cordelia, but, before she could begin to speak, Georgiana spoke instead.

"My Lord, I believe that, at this point, I am best placed to answer that question. Oh, I know it may seem strange to you that a young Lady of my age should say so, but I have, since my father's death, put all of my attention into learning the management of my estates, and discovering what father had planned, and why. Whilst I have focused mainly on Casterfield Grange, amongst his notes and the records there has been much to see of his management of Tillingford."

Gerald, fully aware, after years at war, of the intelligence and capability of a determined woman, accepted her at her word, earning himself Georgiana's eternal respect. For the next few hours, the conversation flowed freely, as they discussed the people and lands of the Tillingford estates, and the previous Baron's policies and attitudes.

Finally, as the dusk closed in outside the windows, the conversation died down. The looked at each other, startled to find the afternoon gone, and smiled in unspoken accord.

Cordelia rang for more refreshments, and sat, feeling more light of heart than she had since her father's death.

"Lord Otford, I must thank you for coming. And you, Baron Setford, for introducing us. I freely admit to you that I was most nervous about this meeting, yet now I find myself fully at ease. I am more grateful than you can know to find that you are a man who can so willingly respect my father's wishes, and who will treat his lands and tenants with the care that they deserve. It is more than I had hoped for. This had been a wonderful afternoon, and I hope that you will see fit to visit us often in the future. Let this be the beginning of a firm friendship." Cordelia's voice was warm and sincere, and Georgiana nodded her agreement.

"Indeed, Otford, this has been an excellent afternoon. Might I suggest that we would be delighted to see you at the celebration of our wedding, in May?"

Gerald found himself agreeing to the Duke's suggestion, and bemused and amazed by the whole experience, took his leave with courtesy, and followed Setford to the carriage. He was stunned to realise that the women genuinely considered him a worthy successor to their father. Him, the man who had done such terrible things during the war, all in the name of keeping their country safe. He could not fathom it, how he could be that terrible man, and the man that they saw, all at the same time.

Deep in thought, he leant back against the padded carriage seat and pondered. Setford, knowingly and wisely, let him be in silence.

Epilogue

The weeks before the wedding, with the girls and Miss Millpost staying at Canterwood Park, had been hectic, and rather eventful, but the day itself dawned clear and bright, the warm spring sunshine and the scent of flowers on the breeze adding to the beauty of the moment.

As Cordelia and the Duke stood in the beautiful old church in the village of Canterwood Downs, the sunlight through the stained-glass windows cast a rainbow over Cordelia's ivory gown, sparking brilliant shimmers of colour off the crystals and seed pearls that adorned it. Finally, the vows were said, and it was done. She felt his lips upon hers, and tears of happiness sprang to her eyes.

In that moment, a sense of great peace descended upon Cordelia. Now, she felt, her father could truly rest – for his fondest wishes had been fulfilled – she was wed, and to his dearest friend. Then the moment passed, and they turned, walking slowly from the church into a swirl of joyous celebration, a cloud of thrown flower petals, and the full warmth of the sun.

By the end of the evening, Cordelia was exhausted, but happy beyond belief. To add to her joy, from what she had seen as the day progressed, her little sister might also finally be on her own path to happiness.

Knowing that lifted the final weight of care from her heart, and she allowed herself to think only of the wonder of having found love with Philip, finding herself care free for the first time since that fateful trip to London over a year ago.

Her fingers entwined with his, she ascended the stairs, more than ready to begin the rest of her life.

The End

(You'll find a taste of book 6, "Redeeming the Marquess" just after the 'About the Author' section in this book!)

Arietta Richmond
Regency Historical Romance

About the Author

Arietta Richmond has been a compulsive reader and writer all her life. Whilst her reading has covered an enormous range of topics, history has always fascinated her, and historical novels been amongst her favourite reading.

She has written a wide range of work, from business articles and other non-fiction works (published under a pen name) but fiction has always been a major part of her life. Now, her Regency Historical Romance books are finally being released. The Derbyshire Set is comprised of 10 shorter novels (6 released so far). The 'His Majesty's Hounds' series is comprised of 10 novels, with the fifth having just been released.

She also has a standalone longer novel shortly to be released, and two other series of novels in development.

She lives in Australia, and when not reading or writing, likes to travel, and to see in person the places where history happened.

Be the first to know about it when Arietta's next book is released!

Sign up to Arietta's newsletter at

http://www.ariettarichmond.com

When you do, you will receive a free copy of the <u>subscriber exclusive</u> novella **'A Gift of Love'**, a prequel to the Derbyshire Set series, which ends on the day that 'The Earl's Unexpected Bride' begins

This story is not for sale anywhere – it is absolutely exclusive to newsletter subscribers!

Here is your preview of

Redeeming the Marquess

His Majesty's Hounds – Book 6

Sweet and Clean Regency Romance

Arietta Richmond

Chapter One

The Berkshire countryside, England, April 1816

Philip Canterwood, Duke of Rotherhithe, surveyed his drawing room with some displeasure.

It was full of a mixed collection of young men, all happy to consume his food, and his excellent wines. He sighed. This was, like it or not, the best to be found as far as eligible young men of noble blood. The ending of the war may have eased things somewhat, but the impact of 20 years of fighting was clearly to be seen. Why was it that it seemed always the best men were the ones to die, and the fools the ones who survived?

He had to hope that at least one of these men was going to suit young Georgiana. They were all of impeccable breeding, titled and supposedly wealthy (although one could never be entirely sure). It was only the quality of their behaviour that gave him concern.

He had promised his bride-to-be's father, on his deathbed, that he would see his younger daughter successfully wed to a man of quality. He intended to fulfil that promise. Unfortunately, she was intelligent, and stubborn – he suspected that, to actually get her to wed, unless a miracle happened, he might have to force her hand. It was not an idea he liked.

Still, a month of these rapacious young men eating his food, and drinking his wine, should give them a suitable chance to impress her – surely, surely, one would take her fancy?

Ah well, he would see soon enough. Cordelia and Georgiana would arrive this evening. He could barely wait to see Cordelia again. He still could not quite believe how lucky he was, to have found love a second time in his life, and with such a beautiful young woman.

He left the young men to their wine and conversation, and went to ensure that all arrangements were in place for his Lady's arrival.

~~~~~

Oliver Kentworth, Marquess of Dartworth, was equally unhappy with the company he found himself in, in the Duke of Rotherhithe's drawing room. Had the opportunity for discussion arisen, the two men would have been surprised to find themselves so much in agreement.

Oliver found the young noblemen who surrounded him to be remarkably shallow and opinionated, without any substance to support those opinions. He felt, unsurprisingly after his last few years, utterly out of place.
~~~~~

He had been surprised to be invited, and was not at all sure that attending had been a wise choice. Time would tell. Given that they were all ignoring him, he suspected that the weeks ahead would not be enjoyable. At the earliest opportunity, he removed himself to the peace of the library.

~~~~~

The mud was thick and wet and stuck to the carriage wheels like sticky, dark molasses.

"If this road becomes any rougher, I am entirely convinced that we shall break a wheel and be stuck in the mud for days and days to come."

Lady Cordelia Branley sighed deeply and looked more than a little seasick as she perched unsteadily inside the rolling carriage and wondered how her beautiful, younger sister could endure the constant jostling and jarring discomfort.

Even more so, she envied Miss Millpost, their long-term companion, her ability to actually sleep under such conditions.

"It can't be much further, Cordelia. An hour at most and we should be at Canterwood Park. I'm sure the road will improve as we get closer."

Georgiana drew a strand of fine blond hair from across her face and smiled at her sister, hoping to cheer her up when she felt no joy herself at leaving her beloved family home.

"I know it's been terribly hard since Papa passed away, dear Cordelia."
~~~~~

The carriage lurched in and out of a deep rut and the two ladies nearly fell off their seats. After a few moments regaining her balance, Georgiana continued speaking.

"And now we have to leave our lovely house so that you can marry the Duke and I can find a husband."

She frowned and pursed her full lips.

"But why on earth did Papa arrange things in such a way? I would never have left the estate if Papa had not placed that annoying clause in his will. It is entirely vexatious to have to marry before I may come into my inheritance fully!"

"Oh, Georgiana. Don't speak of Papa in such a way. He was only thinking of our happiness. He knew it would be difficult for us to manage on our own and only wanted to be sure that we both found good husbands."

The evening was drawing in and a shadow fell across the delicate curve of Georgiana's fine cheekbones. Cordelia gasped as the carriage lurched once again. She was feeling tired and was worried about her appearance after the arduous coach journey. She wanted to look her best for her future husband.

"I, for one, am grateful for my good fortune. I have not only found love, but I am to be the Duchess of Rotherhithe. You know that the Duke is a very kind and wealthy man. He will take very good care of your inheritance until such time as you are married."

Georgiana pulled the carriage blanket about her and shook her head.

"I know I could have taken care of everything myself. With or without a husband!"

Cordelia was slightly shocked at her sister's unladylike sense of independence.

Whilst she had to admit that Georgiana had shown remarkable dedication to learning everything that she could about estate management, in the months since their father's death, she still could not quite comprehend why Georgiana would *want* to do everything herself.

"Papa only wanted the best for you, Georgie, and you know that you can return to the house whenever you want, once you have a new husband - just as soon as you've spoken your wedding vows."

"But your dear Duke has already appointed a farm manager to help the estate manager run Casterfield Grange in our absence and he's even sent over another gardener to look after the grounds. I only hope that they know enough between them to make sure that my flower beds are properly tended. I've worked so hard to cultivate the rose bushes and now a pair of complete strangers are trampling all over my precious flowers in their muddy boots. It just isn't fair!"

"Philip is more than a Duke, Georgiana. Unlike many titled men, he actually cares about his lands and people, just like Papa did. He understands these things. He knows how to run an estate. He's been doing it for years."

"Well, he's certainly had enough years of practice." There was a slightly hard, sulky edge to Georgiana's voice.

Philip Canterwood, the Duke of Rotherhithe, was nearly twenty-five summers older than Cordelia, and Georgiana, in her tiredness was not so subtly referring to that fact.

A silence fell between the two sisters as the cool, damp air pinched at their cheeks and made them pull their carriage blankets closer to their chins.

"Oh Delia, I do worry about you sometimes. I know that you say you love the Duke, and I'm sure you do, but really, are you quite sure about marrying a man so much older than you?"

"Oh course, silly. I do love him, very much, and he loves me. And he's such a sweet and kind gentleman - I just know in my heart that I'm going to be happy with him."

"But he's already an old man, dearest sister. Doesn't that concern you in any way?"

Cordelia laughed.

"He's not so old you know. Forty-two isn't really old. He's in the prime of life — he's strong and handsome, and well respected. Why would that worry me? And... younger men are somehow better? Is that what you're implying?"

Georgiana had no practical experience on the subject of the quality of men, so she simply looked down at the carriage floor.

The carriage bounced and shuddered along the rutted, muddy highway.

Miss Millpost snored gently, propped against the corner of the seat.

"Papa said it was always better to be an old man's sweetheart than a young man's plaything!"

Georgiana looked thoughtful at that, then shrugged.

"I don't think I want to be anyone's sweetheart or plaything. I just want to go home. How long am I really expected to stay at the Duke's, Cordelia? It's such a terrible nuisance to be wrenched away from home like this. Surely, once your wedding is done, I can go home, even if I haven't found anyone to marry by then?"

"I'm sure you'll find someone to marry. Papa left the house and the farmlands to you, Georgiana. He was a Baron and you're a Baron's daughter. You're quite the catch, you know – there will be gentlemen falling at your feet, given that you have a rich dowry, and you're pretty. The house and the lands will be yours as soon as you're wedded, and, even though they will stay yours, as Papa willed it, your new husband will get the benefit of the good income the property will produce. It really couldn't be simpler. Your fate, my darling sister, is in your own hands – you just have to get on with choosing a man and marrying him. And Philip will make sure that you make a good match." Cordelia smiled, with all the warmth her heart could muster in the cramped conditions of the draughty coach.

The unspoken truth was that so many young men of noble blood had taken service in His Majesty's forces to fight the French, and never come home, that there was, to some extent, rather a shortage of eligible young men.

The wars had dragged on for nearly twenty years and the Army and Navy had swallowed up a generation of young men, despatching them to fight in so many wars in faraway places. Whilst the war was now ended, over its course it had taken many, many lives - by disease, musket fire, cannon volleys and the cuts and slashes of sabre blades.

Many young women despaired of ever finding a husband at all, especially a man with all his limbs and eyes intact, who was still on the right side of sixty. Yes, there were still eligible bachelors to be found, but the competition for strong-limbed, blue-blooded and landed young men was fierce indeed. Too many of the young men from the great houses, who had managed to return from war unscathed, or escaped its touch altogether, were more inclined to squander their fortunes at the gaming tables, drinking and carousing, all too aware of how short and cruel life could be.

They preferred to play rather than apply themselves to the arduous business of running their estates. Georgiana felt instinctively repelled by such callow behaviour. She would much prefer to remain on her own than be saddled with some crowing fool who only sought the pleasures of brandy and cards in the smoke-filled salons of disreputable hostesses. It really was a fate too terrible to contemplate. The thought sometimes made her weep with frustration. There had to be a better way – it was so unfair that women were expected to be ruled in all things by men.

In the growing darkness of the carriage's cramped interior, Georgiana's thoughts strayed to the days of her childhood, when life had been far simpler and easier to deal with.

She wished things were simple now. She wished she were back at Casterfield Grange, the house she loved and the lands she'd grown up on, the rich agricultural farm lands she'd learned to care for, and manage. The girls had lost their mother when they were small children; Georgiana had been only five and her sister seven at the time.

Although there had been beautiful portraits of her on the wall of Tillingford Castle, which now graced the halls of Casterfield Grange, neither of the girls could really remember their mother.

The society beauty who had become the dazzling Baroness Tillingford was a faint memory of warm arms and the scent of roses, but little more. They'd had nurses, governesses, maids and companions. But no mother.

Yet both girls had been most fortunate to inherit their mother's fine looks. The early loss of their mother had drawn the two sisters into a close and unbreakable bond of kinship. Cordelia, the taller of the two, had always been deeply fond of her little sister. She'd always felt very protective towards her. She also wondered, sometimes, if the absence of a mother had made Georgiana a little too headstrong and stubborn for a Lady of her rank and position.

But Georgiana was an intelligent young woman with a quick mind and an extremely capable brain. Her father had happily indulged her interest in books by hiring Miss Millpost, a strict but perceptive woman, as governess, and then a tutor to teach her something of the classics. Miss Millpost had spotted a kindred soul in the young child and happily taught her chess, encouraging the curious and critical young mind to flourish and develop in ways that might have shocked the other members of the local aristocracy.

Miss Millpost was a stickler for propriety, but also saw no reason that a girl shouldn't use her brain. In general, girls were expected to sew and learn domestic arts like embroidery, painting watercolours, playing musical instruments, and managing the day to day activities of a household.

Often, women of rank were not even expected to be able to read, in the more traditional of families. There were servants and maids and footmen to attend to all of the manual labours, and a Lady was expected to rule her household with firmness and disciplined good order.

She was not expected to get her delicate fingers dirty or spoil her fine gowns in the gardens. Georgiana had always been a poor fit for that image of womanhood.

She had preferred the outdoors, the stables and the gardens, collecting an impressive variety of plants and flowers. She loved to rush into her father's study with an armful of blooms, mud on her dress and feet, hands grubby from toiling in the soil and place the fragrant petals before him.

He would laugh and kiss her on her forehead and call her his pretty peasant girl, loving her light and energy and indulging her hobbies and interests. She reminded him so much of his deceased wife, who had been just such a bright and intelligent person, if not, perhaps, quite so prone to acquiring a covering of dust or mud on her clothing!

When Miss Millpost had arrived at Casterfield Grange to school Georgiana in the basics, she was also expected to coach her in the ways of gentility. In that area, she would later admit that she wasn't quite as successful as she'd originally hoped. She had imparted good advice along with the daily lessons.

"You might have to disguise your wits, young lady, for an intelligent woman is seen as both a rarity and a novelty and therefore something to be feared. But never abandon them, for they are a rare enough gift either in men or in women!"

Georgiana had studied hard and learned to appreciate her governess's warmth and encouragement, despite her strict and formal presence as they explored the Baron's extensive library. Miss Millpost had agreed to stay with them, as companion now, rather than governess, until Georgiana was married. Shortly before the Baron died he had informed her that he had settled on her, in his will, a substantial annuity, and a cottage, in thanks for her long service. Both Cordelia and Georgiana suspected that Miss Millpost looked forward to the day of Georgiana's marriage with substantial enthusiasm, simply because it would free her to live her own life.

If she had her way, Georgiana fully intended to persuade the Duke simply to give her inheritance and let her run the lands and the household on her own, rather than forcing her to marry before she could do anything. She knew that she was more than capable. She just had to persuade the Duke to see sense. She'd studied hard and understood the rules of agriculture, bookkeeping, finance and how people could flourish when relieved from poverty and oppression. Her father had always treated his tenants well, and she had seen, at first hand, how much impact that had on their lives and their productivity.

Georgiana was completely convinced that she could run her estate successfully, that she could manage the household perfectly well and make sure that the workers and tenants were properly fed and cared for. Her ideas would, most likely, never find favour with her neighbours in the surrounding estates, but she had learnt so much from Miss Millpost, from her private tutor, and from the estate manager, that she now felt a deep responsibility towards the people who lived and worked on her lands.

She only wanted a chance to prove her worth and the only obstacle to that ambition was her sister's future husband, the Duke himself.

Whilst she had to admit that she liked the man, and that he had her best interests at heart, she was also certain that he would do his utmost to abide by her Papa's last wishes. She also had to admit that she had never really demonstrated her ability in his presence – for, until her Papa's death, she had not truly known her own heart, and had simply learned for the joy of it, with no particular purpose in mind. It was quite reasonable that he currently perceived her as a somewhat scatter-brained, if intelligent, girl.

The idea of returning to her wonderful house at Casterfield Grange as the wife of some half-wit, pretentious young nobleman from the local gentry sent shivers of dread down her spine.

At last, they approached the line of handsome poplars which marked the boundary of the Duke's estate, and Cordelia leaned out of the carriage window to catch sight of the lanterns shining atop the magnificent wrought iron gates that were being swung open to admit them. She admired the elegant gatehouse and noted the liveried servants bowing to her as the carriage passed along the gravel driveway that led to the stately house, slowing to a more comfortable pace as the coachman eased the horses to a walk.

This was her moment. She was coming to her new home. She was to be the new Duchess of Rotherhithe, with all of the lands, titles and privileges came with marriage to Philip Canterwood, Duke of Rotherhithe.

Her share of her father's inheritance would add to the Canterwood fortune (although part would always be hers alone, as per the conditions of her father's will) and the two families would be united forever.

The only minor obstacle now, to her complete happiness, was to find a suitable match for Georgiana, her beautiful, headstrong little sister.

The wedding, due to be held just a few short weeks from now, had provided a perfect opportunity to invite every eligible bachelor of noble blood, in the Duke's very wide circle of acquaintance, to a house party, leading up to the celebration. Surely there would be enough handsome young men for one of them to catch Georgiana's fancy, and, she was certain, the Duke would lend a hand in making sure that the right man was chosen. It was the least he could do to please his pretty young bride.

Her own was a match made in heaven and Cordelia was determined that her sister should have the same happiness, and be at the altar within six months of her own wedding - whatever it might take to achieve that.

Georgiana was not the only member of the Branley family with a stubborn streak!

Get

"Redeeming the Marquess"

as soon as it's released – go to http://www.ariettarichmond.com

and make sure that you are signed up for news and release notices!

Books in the 'His Majesty's Hounds' Series

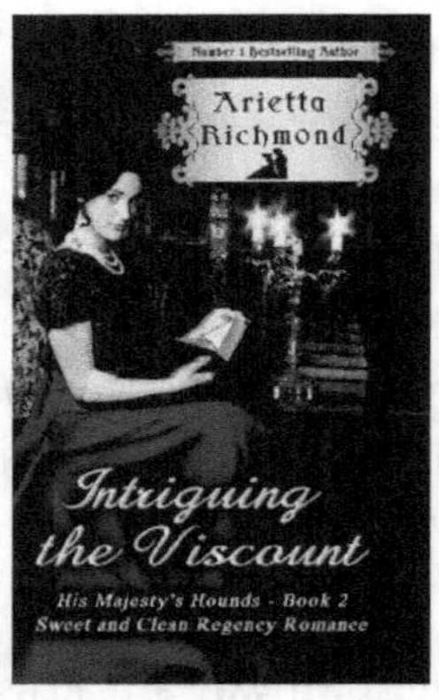

Redeeming the Marquess (coming
soon)

Healing Lord Barton (coming soon)

Winning the Merchant Earl (coming soon)

Loving the Bitter Baron (coming soon)

Rescuing the Countess (coming soon)

Attracting the Spymaster (coming soon)

Books in 'The Derbyshire Set'

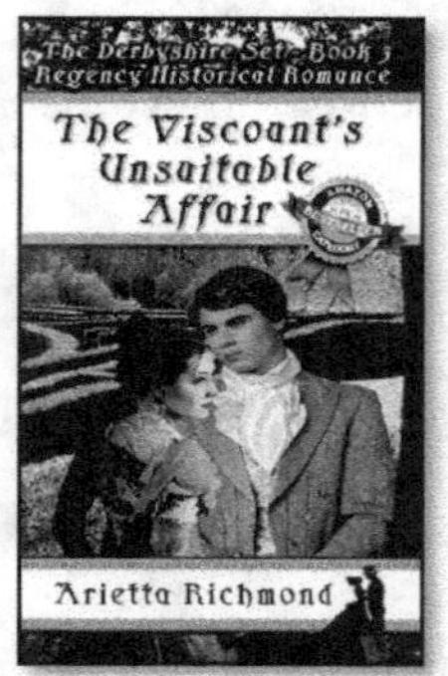

Available at all good book stores and for ebook readers too!

Coming Soon!

Regency Collections with Other Authors

Other Books from Dreamstone Publishing

Dreamstone publishes books in a wide variety of categories – here are some of our other bestselling books:-

We have books in many categories, ranging from Erotica and Romance to Kids Books, Books on Writing, Business Books, Photography, Cook Books, Diaries, Coloring books and much more. New books are released each month.

Be the first to know when our next books are coming out

Be first to get all the news – sign up for our newsletter at

http://www.dreamstonepublishing.com

www.ingramcontent.com/pod-product-compliance
Lightning Source LLC
Chambersburg PA
CBHW071827190726
48292CB00005B/1644